RAYMOND GREINER

HINTERLAND
Journal

TOM: THANK YOU, SO MUCH,
FOR HELPING ME WITH MY
WRITING. WE SHARE A
PASSION TO WRITE. SO NICE.
   RAYMOND

R. Greiner

outskirtspress
DENVER, COLORADO

This is a work of fiction. The events and characters described herein are imaginary and are not intended to refer to specific places or living persons. The opinions expressed in this manuscript are solely the opinions of the author and do not represent the opinions or thoughts of the publisher. The author has represented and warranted full ownership and/or legal right to publish all the materials in this book.

Hinterland Journal
All Rights Reserved.
Copyright © 2015 Raymond Greiner
v1.0

Cover Photo © 2015 thinkstockphotos.com. All rights reserved - used with permission.

This book may not be reproduced, transmitted, or stored in whole or in part by any means, including graphic, electronic, or mechanical without the express written consent of the publisher except in the case of brief quotations embodied in critical articles and reviews.

Outskirts Press, Inc.
http://www.outskirtspress.com

ISBN: 978-1-4787-4295-1

Outskirts Press and the "OP" logo are trademarks belonging to Outskirts Press, Inc.

PRINTED IN THE UNITED STATES OF AMERICA

Contents

Fiction

Pilgrims of Tranquility 1
An Urban Diary 13
Arkansas Reset 24
Battery Acid Wine 37
Finding Level 41
Goat Power 57
Myrna's Story 68
Foxfire 81
The Technology of Nature 86
Ruby Red 97
The Blues 114
Transformation 130
Wolf Spirit 144

Non-Fiction

A Place to Live 153
An Ascetic Life 156
Our Relationship to the Future 159
The Grace of Companionship 162
Consumption 166

Eco-logical	170
Endangered	174
Essentials	177
Falling Back To Butterflies	180
Fringe Benefits	184
Intentional Geometry	187
Goats In The Garden	191
Pond Food	192
The Conundrum of Poverty	195
Winter Solstice 2010	199
Rapa Nui	203
The Nature of Relationships	208
The Last Dogwatch	212
The Necessity To Transform	216
Winter Birds	219
An Echo From The Stars	221
Shadows of Time	229
The Puzzlement of Ancient Spirituality	231
Nature Speaking	234
Remembering Uncle J.P.	237
Techno Logic	245

Hinterland Journal

Hinterland:"An area far from cities, back country."

My home is on 12 acres in southern, rural Indiana, surrounded by woods and fields living in a small cabin 1000 feet from a lightly traveled country road. I look in every direction and see only forest. There is a beautiful small pond, with a walking trail encircling the property. It's a quiet place; I cannot hear the few vehicles passing on the road only sounds of nature.

The concept of one living in solitude is a fascination evoking a variety of images, often of a hermit like character. Is a line drawn separating solitude from isolation? Writers and artists refer to the power of solitude as a means of creative inspiration, others may view living in such a manner as an escape from rigors of social orientations or disorientations. The resolute urbanized, socially interactive person may view solitude as imprisonment. The concept of solitude yields an array of identities, opinions and designs.

Pertaining to myself, solitude has appeared as a direction, neither escape nor method of enlightenment but a position planted from unfolding personal events. Discovery may manifest within solitude, opening more profound ability to reach within, but I don't seek isolationism, nor to become a hermit

HINTERLAND JOURNAL

or "turn key" to my own prison cell. Thoreau spent less time in solitude than typically perceived. His cabin was near town and evening meals were taken at his mother's home, she was a superb cook. He also spent quantities of time at the Lyceum speaking and listening to others. Are we ever totally alone? Society, bonding and friendships touching our lives open thoughts equal to solitude. One's choice of solitude is best accessed as a place of visitation not a place of permanence; although, there are comforts living on the fringe of the present day culture, observing and selecting degrees of interactivity.

As a young man I was drawn to urban life, cities were exciting, but now less desirable. A one-day city experience is quite enough. Nature, and its many nuances of life have always held a position within my deeper self, now occupying my impetus of living. It's a heart felt thrill to observe the variety of life nature offers, immersing in wildness. I am not a philosopher, never studied it, and never cared to study it. I am an observer, with opinions, thoughts and desire to express. As we human bees travel from blossom to blossom a certain amount of pollen sticks. This journal is a collection of stories and essays inspired from a variety of experiences through my readings, life's experiences and walk with nature.

Raymond Greiner

Fiction

Pilgrims of Tranquility

My name is Caleb. I am sixteen years old and documenting my life thus far. I have no parents or siblings. I was scientifically created and live in a barracks facility among one hundred males my age with an adjacent facility housing one hundred females. We are genetically engineered. Guides define goals to expand population. I am inspired to record this eventful, historic time.

It has been two hundred years since global devastation ceased creating present day conditions. Our population expansion team is assigned to Peace School located in a central region of what was previously the United States of America. Currently this country does not exist. History dominates our curriculum intending to circumvent repetition of events nearly destroying all earthly life. Even after two hundred years residue from this cycle of destruction hinders restructuring. Events occurring over two hundred years ago were unimaginable.

The United States bears responsibility as the primary source of stimulation for catastrophic events. This allegation is because the United States represented a position of prominence during this era. Social erosion slowly developed within the country predominantly from extreme leadership inefficiency. Large industrial enterprise and banking controlled

HINTERLAND JOURNAL

government disregarding welfare of the general population. Corruption infiltrated all levels of government culminating in tangled misdirection. The United States economy fragmented imposed by greed oriented profit objectives through relocating major manufacturing facilities to foreign locations, exploiting economically depressed countries offering lower cost labor. This endeavor diminished American middle class tax revenue leading to fiscal collapse. United States consumption fell dramatically negatively impacting foreign enterprise and manufacturing dependent on American consumerism resulting in global economic decline. Simultaneously Muslim extremists threatened war with subversive bombings seizing opportunity caused by a weakened economy to inflict further damage. Lacking tax revenue United States defense systems were reduced; although, maintaining and escalating atomic weaponry conjecturing extremists would be constrained yielding to fear of these weapons. Then a triggering event occurred. A Muslim country developed nuclear weaponry aspiring to use these weapons against the United States. New York City was reduced to ashes. Immediately the United States began launching nuclear missiles, randomly bombing Muslim countries, reacting without clear knowledge which Muslim country was responsible for the nuclear attack. This action resulted in global, anti-American nuclear powers to view the United States as a wounded lion, emulating jackals and hyenas, pouncing on this much-hated country. North Korea destroyed the west coast entirely and also Japan, an ally of the United States. The tipping point was breached igniting a frenzy of relentless atomic attacks as the United States unleashed every missile in its arsenal. Washington DC was annihilated and United

PILGRIMS OF TRANQUILITY

States leadership was gone. The nuclear attacks killed millions, destruction far beyond what could have been imagined. Only those in isolated geographic locations survived and millions more died over the next year from radioactive fallout. Nuclear winter developed and many froze to death. Populations became sterile, some living another five years developing cancer or other health failures from extreme radiation exposure. Most early deaths were from starvation. Food production stopped, without transport. The world never experienced such horror and despair. Bedlam dominated; among the few survivors food acquisition was the highest priority, with much of the remaining food contaminated from the attacks. Clans formed in an attempt to survive but failed quickly from either killing each other or starvation. The country was nearly void of human life six years after the attacks as greater numbers died after the attacks than during the attacks. The United States became a barren landscape. The recurring atomic explosions damaged the ozone producing erratic weather patterns weakening the atmosphere allowing meteor penetration with frequent strikes throughout the world. In an intense final stance the United Stated destroyed North Korea and Muslim countries were in ruin. Some areas of the world felt less impact. Hunger was widespread; countries not directly hit slowly regained order.

 Our group's foundation was formed by an alliance of surviving countries in an attempt to discover new direction for population expansion seeking social design engendering higher ethical standards void of propensity for supremacy, which historically provokes war and its consequence.

 Teacher Benedict: "Good morning to all of you. It has been my great honor to serve as your teacher to this point in your journey into the future. The alliance has worked nearly one hundred years striving to arrive at this time. Studies and analysis during early stages concluded social order lost balance with Earth, beginning in the Fertile Crescent representing the genesis of humankind's thirst for conquest using war as its means. Population growth and border establishment initiated confrontational opportunities. Sumer had a standing army as early as 3000 BCE, a composite leading to the brink of human extinction."

"Artifacts of ancient cultures disclose less confrontational and societal dysfunction. Neanderthal tribes lived harmoniously for three hundred thousand years. Very early social orders were not plagued with high population densities intensifying complexities. Hunter-gatherer tribes displayed social compatibility, embracing earthly cycles in cadence with nature."

"Alliance planners envision an experiment and those of you sitting here today represent the beginning toward discovering a more peaceful future. Until now your curriculum concentrated on historical events leading to warring eras. From this point forward you will be encouraged to interact socially establishing male/female partnerships. You have been raised as a unit offering insight toward developing lifetime partnerships. You have studied and worked together in preparation to confront your future. The alliance constructed five communes located within various geographic temperate zones using geodesic dome structures to house partners allowing space to expand to a family of four. Twenty residents will occupy each commune. This design replicates ancient social grouping melding with limited modern conveniences. One partnership assigned to each commune will receive medical training and properly equipped to provide health services. During formative years you were assigned daily to work in the school's vegetable garden learning techniques of gardening. Gardening will become your routine. Each household will raise a garden with a larger garden shared by communal members and garden yields will represent your single source of food. You will have no weapons and killing animals is forbidden. Your scientifically created genetic profiles were carefully planned establishing character traits obtained from selective sources emphasizing a combination" "of qualities. These qualities include love, compassion, work ethic and intelligence combining with natural non-confrontational behavior. During your communal experience you will have access to technological devices and a daily journal will be maintained communicating with the alliance. This daily record will be assigned to one individual; however, all participants are encouraged to document thoughts conveying them to the alliance as a method of enhancing future programs."

Teacher Benedict was correct regarding our bonding, we knew each other far exceeding typical and daily physical work formed trust and respect. Since my earliest years I have been very close with a female member, her name is Marlene and she is strikingly beautiful. We engaged in long discussion for as long as I can remember. One experience is vivid in my memory. We were seven years old and just beginning to learn gardening. Marlene happened upon a garter snake and became extremely frightened. I picked up the snake explaining it was harmless and she need not fear it. She looked at me in an odd manner but said nothing. A few days later she beckoned me to the storage shed. Inside the shed was a box with five garter snakes.

HINTERLAND JOURNAL

"I captured these garter snakes so we can share their release. It will be delightful to see them regain freedom. I don't fear them since you taught me they are harmless."

This event became fixed in my mind. Although simple and seemingly of little importance the incident revealed Marlene's heart and natural connection to nature and its functions. She overcame fear through knowledge and understanding displaying compassion. We shared profound love and closeness, craving deeper connection. We agreed our life together would be meaningful living with fellow students taught by alliance guides. We became partners venturing forward.

After the selection process we were transported to assigned commune sites. We were not given an exact location only told it was south of where we were born and trained. The average yearly temperature and rainfall were major factors selecting locations. Upon arrival the domes were in place with ample space for gardening and also a larger dome to serve as common space for gatherings. Dwellings were furnished, including two computers allowing opportunity to communicate with alliance leaders and guides. Two natural springs flowed through the area and a well with a hand pump was installed. The alliance provided a year's supply of food while our group establishes self-reliance. An array of solar panels supplied power with satellite connection relaying computer-transmitted messages to the alliance. In our communal garden we will grow hemp to be stored, accumulated and processed as material for clothing. It seemed possible to be self-sufficient within this arrangement.

Soon day-to-day functions fell in place and Marlene and I felt escalated to a higher plane. It was a glorious feeling, compatible in every manner of living. No government controls were applied. Our group met frequently in the common area for discussions toward achieving sustainability. Work sharing became routine. Much labor was required making compost for soil enrichment; cutting firewood for cooking and heat. Communal unity heightened the entire undertaking.

Alliance message: "The combined opinion of alliance members is one of great pride and appreciation for the sincere effort your group exhibits. You have been given a title. You are referred to by our alliance as 'Pilgrims of"

"Tranquility'. As you progress personal gratitude will expand, inspired by physical efforts revealing higher self awareness, an element largely lost within what was historically termed 'modern society' shunning physical chores. Frugality attached to manual tasking allows sensory capacities to permeate your lives, elevating introspection, enhanced by environmental dynamics. Materialism is absent in your regimen. This experiment strives to gain knowledge regarding humankind's ability to blend less intrusively with the Earth applying minimal, amiable practices. Although premature for accurate analysis we are encouraged at this early stage."

Marlene's message to the Alliance: "Caleb and I have become intensely attached while adjusting to communal life. We feel fortunate and grateful to be given this opportunity."

"In our discussions questions have arisen. From our historical studies previous to communal placement it was revealed how global ethical standards and values slowly eroded. This erosion was not solely government indiscretion; the collective society was mired in dysfunction far adrift from principles taught by our mentors and teachers. Our experimental group was scientifically created choosing selective gene banks. We were taught from our earliest memories the importance of high personal standards, emphasizing peaceful coexistence and altruism, combined with simplicity. It is apparent to the alliance and also apparent to those of us participating in this experiment that absence of these characteristics bore responsibility for mayhem destroying much earthly life. Our root question is: How has this changed? It is unrealistic to imagine global populations scientifically created on a large scale, duplicating our guidance and learning. Has society made progressive adjustments toward betterment? Does anger, hate and war mentality" "remain? Are selfishness and greed continuing during restructuring? If so, how will our small scale experimental lifestyles implement sweeping change?"

"We agree our simplistic life, tending crops, embracing basic elements of living offers higher personal balance; however, studying the historic failure period reveals these elements were not in place and without recognition. Materialism and monetary status formed a God like presence creating ubiquitous corruption touching all levels of social structure. Cities infested with crime, poverty and social separation as the wealthy lolled in extreme comfort pressing toward gain beyond necessity and those with less were ignored and often chastised. It seems unlikely to us our example can alter such large scale historic revelations."

Alliance: "Marlene, your points of discussion are worthy, meriting response. Since inception the alliance has addressed these issues becoming an ongoing debate regarding the experiment's long-term viability. Currently many oppose the alliance and its goals. Our purpose is to learn what results can be achieved evaluating future applications based upon degree of proven worth. Social restructuring is not reflecting teachings you and your fellow pioneers received. During the rebuilding cycle repetition of dysfunctional activity during the historic self-destructive period regained momentum. Although, no major wars have erupted and atomic weaponry is absent. Anger, mistrust and convoluted disposition have returned. Selfishness, greed and materialistic goals have reemerged. We agree it is not a feasible solution to attempt genetic engineering on a large scale, quite an impossible task, creating uncertainty regarding progress. However, we do sense headway via this communal demonstration. If social order continues downward, again becoming destructive, your group will demonstrate value as harbingers;" "exhibiting peaceful coexistence is possible. Your success is germinating seeds of change. The alliance's philosophy and purpose is presently a minority view with limited range of acceptance, which may ultimately lead to failure. Your group is nearing self-sufficiency and if our alliance is broken your commune will become a beacon, lighting a better course away from social flaws. Your group shows alternative to the 'grab bag' of materialism. The vista is clouded at this point, but as time passes it is possible that your precedent exhibiting solidarity, compassion and self-sustainability may be just enough to tip the scale exposing proof that cannot be ignored. It is our hope. The looming reality is humanity must change if longevity is to be attained. It cannot endure cycle after cycle of destructiveness."

    My name is Caleb. I am forty-five years old, documenting my life thus far. I was scientifically created and have no parents or siblings. I was created to participate in an experiment

HINTERLAND JOURNAL

forming a new approach to human development. I have a loving partner Marlene, who is the stalwart supporter of my life and equally responsible for our achievements. Our teachers and mentors were organized by an alliance offering opportunity to prove peaceful, compatible life is possible aspiring toward symmetrical coherence with Earth. The alliance that formed us failed, caused by reemergence of social dysfunction that nearly destroyed humanity; however, participants in this new design of peaceful coexistence succeeded and remain. Established partnerships grew into families and our communal concept spilled over influencing others away from dysfunctional social function. Our new approach expanded beyond what many predicted. Without alliance support we progressed, gaining knowledge, building shelters from natural materials opening opportunity for expansion duplicating patterns of our success. Even though materialistic, dominating society continues some are becoming influenced by our simplistic life discovering worth outside overt consumption and control. Those participating in the foundation of this new direction are gratified. We had dubious thoughts of success but encouraged by teachings during alliance years. The alliance named us "Pilgrims of Tranquility" and now we are many.

The alliance spoke of the necessity for humanity to discover equanimity or perish and this wisdom has proven correct and moving to its future.

From Marlene's journal: "I am communicating with students entrapped in the old convoluted culture. They admire our effort but plagued with skepticism. Some feel humanity is incapable of large-scale change embracing our model, perceiving the pursuit of dominance as an inbred human trait.

PILGRIMS OF TRANQUILITY

Questing power over those viewed as weaker spawns from instinctual mechanisms derived from the axiom of survival of the fittest. From our philosophical viewpoint displaying wealth and dominance as superiority forms false perception of balance, graphically obvious in wealth worshiping cultures. Within this concept the most fiscally affluent are distinguished, recognized as the most revered. My argument is, as with all earthly life forms, humans adjust to environmental conditions. If social development instills the shallowness of materialism this design becomes broadly accepted. Through teachings by alliance mentors our cohesiveness opens new direction enhancing purpose. Dominance is absent, we have no monetary system, and wealth is not recognized with the same ascendency as the historically destructive culture. Our ability to work in simplistic union, sharing subsistence efforts represents wealth. We are master gardeners, students of the Earth and its myriad of mannerisms. We view fellow communal members equally without necessity for individual power and control."

"It is encouraging to see so many joining us bringing added dimension to the commune's structure and future. In our curriculum at Peace School it was taught that even during the high point of the destruction period a minority sought peace, but were overwhelmed by warring forces, driven by intent to dominate. This knowledge reveals similarities to our philosophy existed during the destructive period."

"Our curriculum did not include exposure the arts or music. Most of us have learned of the joys of music and art using our computers. Recently a young man appeared from the woods after a very long trek to locate us. He was carrying a guitar and serenaded us in the common area dome. This event

HINTERLAND JOURNAL

was extraordinary, a spiritual awakening. A former alliance member has become our benefactor as much as he is able. He shipped us twenty guitars and now the musician appearing in our lives is our teacher and we are experiencing great joy from learning to play the guitar. It is such a wonderful feeling."

Epilogue: The five communes established by the alliance remain intact. Learning has been expansive and continuing, integrating with those seeking change from historic social flaws. It is unknown if this proven harmonious culture can expand, creating global balance. The communes have maintained their original direction based upon early teachings as additional residents opened freshness, with music bringing dimension to the pilgrim's mission.

So, the world is at a crossroad, option to chaos has manifested. Life in the commune is tuned to the Earth and its natural functions, synchronizing with universal consciousness. Humankind evolved in concert with Earth's tides, then strayed nearly destroying itself. Nature's vast, immeasurable patterns of progression must be embraced in order to secure humanity's future. Alternatives are infinite in nature's progressive timeline, continually adjusting. The voice of destiny sings in varied rhythmic tones, often off key and out of tempo, like a catbird singing in a thorn bush. Then the sky opens and darkness becomes light as clouds of doubt vanish. The Pilgrims of Tranquility have unfolded an Earth story.

An Urban Diary

I awaken to the hydraulic whine of a trash truck. Nearby a massive waste incinerator emits a polluting stench mixing with the incessant rumble of traffic.

Detroit, once a grand city, is in steep decline with eroding tax revenue caused by urban flight becoming stagnated in residue of its past. Littered streets with blocks of abandoned homes occupied by vagrants and drug addicts. These vacant homes are windowless, empty remnants of thriving neighborhoods.

My apartment is above a bar clinging to its few remaining customers, since most commute resisting over indulgence for their nightly drive. A few young professionals wander in for happy hour a beginning of their ritual, daily mind numbing to be continued nearer home at a more affluent place. I go in for a beer on occasion, it's a fascination to observe patron's character posturing as they mingle displaying vogue fashion and language in an effort to present themselves as centerpieces of attention.

A homeless man scavenges the dumpster in the ally each night prior to the trash truck's arrival. I talk with him on occasion, he never asks for money, impresses me somewhat and his name is Joe. He's an untypical homeless person, bright eyed, a quick mind and clean in appearance, although his dress defines his homeless status. Joe told me he was a Vietnam vet awarded the Bronze Star with a combat V for bravery and he had worked for 10 years at an automobile factory, was married, had two children and his life was classic mainstream until the factory closed leaving him jobless. His wife divorced him and his two grown children shun him. He divided his savings among his children as they each turned eighteen then gradually his life unwound into despair. He became consumed with alcohol then quit drinking after his best friend died of liver failure and he told me his life is now much better than most could imagine. I enjoyed talking with Joe; he revealed warmth and an articulate tone with a surprising vocabulary. I was comfortable with Joe.

I teach engineering and math at Wayne State University and have yet to participate in "white flight", always enjoyed metropolitan life with memories lingering of a vibrant city in the early seventies when I began teaching at Wayne. My classes are scheduled early and I habitually walk to my apartment since it is still daylight. Venturing on the streets of Detroit after dark is risky and should be avoided. One day I saw Joe walking toward me wearing a backpack, and was striding along at a good pace. I stopped and addressed him.

"Hey Joe, how are you doing."

"Hello Allen, I didn't recognize you at first. I'm doing fine, just came from the YMCA. I go there almost every day, exercise and get a shower. I'm headed for the library; it's usually my second stop after the Y. I am taking online college courses using the library's computers."

"Joe, how about me buying you lunch tomorrow, we can meet in at the campus cafeteria, I get a discount. I have a three

AN URBAN DIARY

o'clock class. We can meet at noon."

"That would be really nice Allen, I can fill you in on details of my life. How things have played out over the past five years."

"Good, see you then."

As Joe departed I lost any sense of his homelessness, detecting no somber, sad eyes or expression of aimlessness depicting loss of purpose. Joe exhibited vibrancy that I seldom see in people I meet day to day.

The next day at noon Joe was waiting at the entrance to the cafeteria building.

"I see you made it, glad you could come"

"I wouldn't miss this, it's not everyday that an old street dweller is invited to lunch by a college professor. I am grateful.

We took trays and made our way through the long line. I noticed Joe did not heap his tray, selecting healthy choices. Joe looked trim and fit with good skin color.

"So, Joe what's your typical day like? It interests me how you function routinely each day."

"During my early times on the street was much different than the present time. I had fallen into an unimaginable, deep and horrible state. My ambition to work or reconnect to mainstream life had been removed from my being. I would have certainly committed suicide, but did not have the nerve to perform the task becoming an empty, wandering person. I was forced to panhandle, and not very successful; it was demeaning, adding anxiety. I begged for food at various places, raided dumpsters at supermarkets and would show up for charitable handouts. Alcohol fueled my life entirely, any money I could beg was used to buy cheap wine offering escape from my misery.

"How did you make the transition to the Joe sitting with me now sharing this meal?"

"Allen, I have no short answer to your question. I'm unsure if I even know myself. It's a classic example of the metaphoric 'baby steps'. After a time I adjusted to street life, made friends with other homeless people. One close friend was also a Vietnam vet suffering from alcoholism. As I told you earlier he died of liver failure in an ally alone. His death had great impact on me, and a desire grew within to seek higher self worth. By this time I had honed my skills as a street survivor. I became eligible to collect social security at age sixty-two giving me a small but important financial base. I also knew that in order to pull my life in a better direction on eight hundred dollars a month would be a daunting challenge. I was accustomed to street life and decided to remain homeless but with alterations from the previous two years. Alcohol was the first to go, which immediately created a higher plane of stability. I bought a backpack, down sleeping bag and a quality small tent. Using acquired knowledge of the city I knew places to sleep that were safe and invisible to criminals and police. My system worked well even during the harshest winter nights. I still use shelters on occasion, especially during extreme weather. I am conjecturing that the first question in your mind is: 'why not leave the city?' This answer is also complex."

"Yes, my first thought, as I visualize the danger of living on the streets of Detroit a crime ridden city on a downward spiral. From my viewpoint it would be my first reaction, relocate geographically, away from this squalid zone."

"I was born and raised in Detroit, and during formative years Detroit was a joyful and exciting city. I remain emotionally connected to this city, and because it is suffering urban decay I can't bring myself to abandon it. I personally know most of the thugs and criminals roaming the streets. They leave me alone, knowing I don't carry money or valuables. I counsel a few young black males trapped in hopelessness. I meet Tyrone Jackson twice a week and am helping him pass online high school courses using the library's computers. This is a step for him to acquire a certified high school diploma allowing opportunity to enter the military. Opportunity is the missing element among inner-city youth. This effort gratifies me and gives Tyrone a sense of purpose lessening his desire to continue as a street thug."

"The condition Detroit has fallen into is a cycle. All earthy composites experience cycles, some are short and some take millions of years to attain fruition. This is evident to me, and I sincerely believe Detroit will heal and re-establish as a vital city again. Many thoughts and experiences have stimulated my direction during this later stage of life. I still function as a homeless person, raid dumpsters and take meals served by charitable groups. I also escaped the city a few days each month during warm seasons. Detroit has a unique and little known connection. Just south of the city is a forty-eight mile stretch along the river, the Detroit River National Wildlife Refuge. This is a magnificent place. I take the bus to the end of its route then hike a short distance to the refuge. Camping is forbidden but I have discovered places where I can camp undetected. Few visit the refuge and it has no active" "enforcement. This place offers wonderful solitude and connection to nature. It's refreshing to be at such a beautiful and remote place."

"I am impressed Joe, we must meet again and discuss more

about your life, future and the direction Detroit must eventually take."

Without awareness Joe had become an ascetic, discovering embracing life simplistically reveals a deeper sense of purpose. All great, historical sages and spiritual leaders used asceticism as a vehicle toward spiritual growth and a higher sense of purpose. The logic is that moving away from affluence allows a more genuine dimension to the human spirit and personal evolutionary consciousness.

I kept track of Joe, tried to contact him once a week. Knowing his routine helped, the YMCA, library and wildlife refuge were habitual places for Joe. One day I dropped by the library. Joe was standing near a bank of computers occupied by four black youths. He was moving from one to the next pointing to the computer's screen and whispering his thoughts to each of his students. Joe told me later at one of our routine lunch meetings that he was making an effort to recruit more black youths to participate in his effort to further their education. He said he has never felt so good in his life; interaction with these underprivileged kids kindled his spirit for living. He became friends with Ms Ambrose the head librarian who had observed Joe develop his student count. One day she called him into her office, and led him to a separate room. She opened the door and inside was twenty desks with a computer on each desk. Ms Ambrose was so impressed with Joe's effort she contacted library benefactors and they purchased these computers to better accommodate Joe's teaching goals. Joe was overwhelmed at this event, and this thoughtful gift stunned him, simultaneously motivating him. Within a short time Joe had a student count of fifty and had to schedule class time. A reporter from the

AN URBAN DIARY

Detroit News wrote an article on Joe and the mayor awarded him a commendation for his efforts. Joe worked tirelessly to recruit students as some passed their high school curriculum and moved on. Joe continued teaching for two years and then became ill with pneumonia and was hospitalized. I volunteered to be Joe's replacement while he recovered. I was delighted to help and visited Joe each day at the hospital keeping him informed regarding his class.

One day while I was monitoring the class a young, sharply dressed army sergeant walked in, introducing himself.

"I am Tyrone Jackson a former student of Joe's. I heard he was ailing and took leave to visit him. How is he doing?"

"Tyrone, this is truly amazing to me, you were Joe's first student. He's doing fine, will be released from the hospital tomorrow and wants to visit with the class. He's not quite ready to teach, needs a few more days to recover, but told me all he thinks about is returning to teaching. Can you stop by and surprise him?"

"Sure, what time."

"I will bring Joe at ten AM."

As I picked up Joe at the hospital, he seemed weak but enthusiastic. Kept rattling on and on about how much he missed teaching.

"I want to go to the class first, then I have a bed at the shelter to finish my recovery. Allen, I cannot express to you how appreciative I am for taking over my class."

As we entered the classroom, the entire class was in a small group and they clapped and cheered when Joe entered. Then hiding behind the group, out walked Tyrone, looking so sharp in his uniform. Joe fell into silence, looked at me, and then looked at Tyrone. Tears flowed from his eyes and he was speechless, as he hugged Tyrone.

Tyrone then addressed the class: "Well, my brothers, what about this? We are the lost tribe of Detroit, trapped in squalor and dysfunction. We are viewed as hopeless, uneducated, bound for a life of crime. Society shunned us, casts us aside as if we were waste products. Then here comes this homeless white guy who knows the degradation and pain of an outcast. Joe rescued us, opened a door that nobody else opened. I was deep into a pit of despair when Joe counseled me and delivered me to a better place. I am forever grateful."

It was all Joe could do to keep his emotions in check. And I invited Tyrone to have lunch with Joe and I. It was one of the most memorable events of my life. Tyrone also told Joe of a young woman he knew who had dropped out of high school because of her pregnancy and wondered if Joe could consider her for his classes. Joe was totally delighted; he had tried earlier to find female students but failed. This had been a long time ambition for Joe.

I retired from Wayne State and moved to Florida. I kept in touch with Joe and he continued his teaching. One day I received a phone call from Ms. Ambrose. Joe had not showed up for his classes for five days. She was worried. She filed a missing person report with the police, and they searched for Joe but were unable to locate him. I told her to check the wildlife refuge and that Joe often camped at the refuge.

The state police found Joe in his tent. He had died from an unknown cause. It was such a sad day for me. I called Ms. Ambrose and told her I would pay for Joe's funeral and asked her to help me with a memorial service to be held at his classroom. Over two hundred of Joe's former students attended, including Tyrone and his wife Cicely. Who would have ever imagined an old homeless man could have positively impacted so many young men and women mired in a pit of hopelessness. My memory drifted back to my last long conversation with Joe. I had just retired and was preparing to move to Florida.

"Joe, how long do you intend to follow this theme you have created? I am impressed at what you have accomplished."

"I've thought about this Allen, and it seems impossible for me to go back or change my life. I have no place to go, no family, and this effort I have made and the results represent the highpoint of my life. When I find my way to the library each day and interact with those kids I feel as if a miracle has descended upon me. Each day offers personal significance and enlightenment. I read about the lady they called Peace Pilgrim. Her name was Mildred Norman and she walked the highways for nearly thirty years promoting peace, often going without food and sleeping in culverts and abandoned buildings. Mildred taught various sagacious principles during speeches and contacts in her travels. One of her quotes struck me. 'Unnecessary possessions are unnecessary burdens. There is great freedom in simplistic living. It is those who" "have enough, but not too much who are the happiest.' I think of her message often. Our present day society is inundated with a drive to amass possessions, viewing money and wealth as God like. Contemporary social design is a glut-oriented facade, placing values amidst status, fused with consumption and accumulation. This design vividly displays social separation as we gauge and classify our fellow beings according to race, income, size and location of homes, cars we drive, and clothes we wear. This overpowering desire for material wealth generates insecurity, falsely perceiving Utopia can be discovered among these trappings. The kids I teach are byproducts of this social condition. They serve no purpose to the masses entrapped in shallow lives engulfed by self-serving goals. My teaching offers these young people hope, purpose and direction. It gives them personal identity and a realization that life is what you make it to be, applying energy and thought, seeking inward growth and meaning. I feel I have enough, but not too much and I am very happy with my life."

After Joe's memorial service Tyrone and his wife Cecily approached me and Tyrone handed me an envelope. The envelope contained a photo of Joe standing behind one of his students at the computer, pointing to the screen. He then said: "Ms Ambrose asked you and I to meet in her office for a few minutes."

We entered Ms. Ambrose's office and sat in front of her desk. She spoke:

"Allen, I have no idea what to do at this point regarding Joe's students and their future. We now have in excess of 100 students and have increased our computer bank to 30 computers. Joe had the" "students on precise schedules using advanced students as interns. This is perplexing and worrisome. Do you have any suggestions?"

As I pondered Ms. Ambrose's conundrum, I thought of my condo in Florida, the daily beach walks, the pristine sidewalks with little signs along the way reminding the old folks "don't walk on the grass" and the multiple neighborhood crime watch warning signs. Life as a retiree in Florida is a mundane affair; most are early risers, go out for coffee and conversation. Little

AN URBAN DIARY

boxes mounted along walkways filled with plastic bags to pick up your dog's poop. Everything nicely structured, with the main event each day to hit the local restaurants for the "early bird special." It's a facile life, much walking, talking and watching TV. As these thoughts passed through my mind I thought of Joe and his belief that life's values exist more profoundly within our hearts and our contributions. I thought of the day I first met Joe pillaging that dumpster, an odd place to discover a saint.

I was awakened by the hydraulic whine of a trash truck. Nearby a large waste incinerator emits a polluting stench mixing with the incessant rumble of traffic. This morning I am grateful to be awakened; I have an early morning class at the library, and two new students to interview.

Arkansas Reset

Matthew Ayres has been an investment banker for twenty years working his way up the ladder of success becoming an officer on the stock exchange. His accumulated personal investments are substantial offering financial security and continuing to expand.

Ayres lives in New York City meeting weekly for lunch with his associate and friend William Hurley, a fellow financial advisor he has known since early in his career.

"Bill, this is Matt lets meet today at that new place the Prosperity Café, on 16th street."

"Good idea, I've been wanting to try it. I'll be there at 12:30."

The Prosperity Café caters to the financial district, a plush restaurant serving gourmet entrées.

"Glad you made it Bill. How are your investments looking lately?"

"Quite good considering the overall economic tenor. Fiscal influence remains the prominent global power. Commodities are all over the place causing concern. Industry is still pumping out consumer goods, which seems to be the stronger factor. I hear and read negative things about food shortages and escalating third world poverty. These issues cycle perpetually. Last night I watched a program featuring a psychic speaking of

ARKANSAS RESET

a soon to occur asteroid strike."

"Psychics make their living predicting doom and gloom. With technology in place today, listening to such talk is a waste of time. If an asteroid is on course to collide with our planet we will know far in advance."

"Those are my thoughts too."

"I want you to accompany me on a fishing trip to the Ozark Mountains in Arkansas, near the Missouri border. I discovered a great lodge on a mountain lake. It would be a nice get away. A change from city environment."

"I would sure enjoy that, I need a break."

Time was arranged and the two bankers drove to Arkansas, since no airports were near the lodge.

They arrived at Paradise Of The Ozarks, a rustic lakeside lodge reflecting pillow white clouds on the lake's glasslike surface, a contrast from New York City. Fred and Barbara Cummings, the lodge owners, greeted them.

"Welcome, I'm Fred and this is Barbara, thank you for choosing our lodge. Your rooms are ready. You will enjoy this area; the fishing is as good as it gets, many trophy bass in this lake. Boats with outboards will be available at your convenience. Meals are served at 7AM and 6PM, with box lunches for fishing excursions. We are at your service."

"I'm Matt, and this is Bill, we are delighted to be here."

Barbara showed the men to their rooms.

"I am available at any time to assist. Just give me a ring."

"What do you think Bill?"

"I think the name is befitting."

At breakfast Fred assisted Barbara and the food was exquisite. Fred directed the men to areas of the lake for the best fishing.

"No new guests expected for a week. You two will have the lake mostly to yourself. You may see my friend Rod, he rows a johnboat, gave up on motors years ago, wears corduroy clothing, explaining this was Thoreau's choice and best for comfort and durability. He may appear odd, but he's an" "exceptional person. He helps me on occasion but refuses payment. He will wave at first, but later will stop and talk. He knows all the holes with the largest bass and will tell you where to catch a trophy. He is a former biology professor, forced to retire from brain injuries when he was struck by lightning on three different occasions. He's the most interesting person I have ever met; although fearful of storms, and lives in a cave. Rod is not his real name; those around here nicknamed him Lightning Rod because of his experiences, later everyone started calling him Rod. His real name is James Markham and is well known in the academic community from books and papers he has written."

Both men were fascinated and looking forward to meeting Rod. They gathered their fishing gear and headed to the boat dock. The lake was mirror calm. The beauty of this place can penetrate one's soul.

They chose a corner of the lake with a grove of hemlocks near the shoreline. As they began casting lures for bass Rod appeared, waving as he rowed passed feathering his oars on each stroke in graceful, fluid motion. He moved to a far section of the lake and anchored. Untypically, he used a short fishing pole. He attached bait and dropped his line over the side of the boat. In a brief time he jerked the pole and out came a lunker bass. He then pulled his anchor and began to row toward the two men.

"Hello fellow anglers. Are you getting any hits? My name is Rod and I have fished this lake for years. I just caught my breakfast."

Matt: "As we observed. No hits yet. What kind of bait are you using?"

"I use brightly colored jigs, they are the best for smallmouth bass. They taste better than the large mouth. I stopped casting lures long ago."

Rod then reached over handing Matt two small jig lures.

"Put a split shot sinker about ten inches up from the jig bait, let it drop to the bottom and then reel in about two feet of line moving the bait up and down slightly every few seconds. You will be amazed. I'll probably see you again tomorrow, you can tell me how it worked out."

"Thanks Rod, we will give it a try."

Rod rowed toward the shore and the two bankers did as instructed. After a few minutes using Rod's technique they each landed a large small mouth bass. This continued until they filled their stringer and headed back to the lodge. Proudly holding their fish showing Fred. Fred responded.

"I see you found Rod, or he found you. He enjoys showing guests his tricky little bass rig. When new guests come in with a stringer like that I know Rod was involved. I'll gut them for you and put them in the freezer, we will cook them later, but not tonight. Barbara is preparing my favorite dish, venison stroganoff. You won't believe this dish, nothing better in New York City, I guarantee."

At dinner both men praised Barbara, they were overwhelmed with this meal. Chunks of venison marinated in wine sauce, tender and uniquely seasoned to enhance flavor, melting in their mouths.

Matt: "Barbara, this is unbelievable, can't recall a meal this tasty. Thank you for your effort giving us this unforgettable meal."

Bill: "I agree Barbara, it's the best ever."

"I enjoy cooking, it's an art form. Tomorrow night I will serve your bass using my special breading formula on the filets."

Fred: "You two can do me a favor tomorrow. I seldom see Rod; since I am stuck here with chores and it is likely you will see him daily. Ask Rod to have dinner with us tomorrow evening. He did some electrical wiring for me, and did a very good job; he's knowledgeable on electrical installations. I need to convert one outlet from single-phase to three-phase and need his advice. I'm certain he will come."

Matt: "Sure, we will enjoy talking with him again."

The next day Rod appeared on the lake near the bankers.

"How did my bass rig perform?"

Matt: "Our stringer was full. Thanks for the tip. Fred and Barbara have invited you for dinner this evening. She's cooking the bass we caught yesterday using her gourmet recipe. Dinner is at seven. Fred wants your advice on an electrical problem."

"I'll sure be there, I enjoy those two."

"Good, see you at seven."

Then Rod rowed quietly away in the direction he came.

Rod showed up at the lodge around six anticipating assisting Fred with his electrical glitch. As Fred and Rod analyzed the electrical complication Barbara prepared the meal. The two executives watched in awe as Rod instructed Fred in the method of converting single-phase electrical current to three-phase, connecting a series of wires and the job was completed quickly.

Barbara summoned the men to the table serving platters of bass filets. The aroma intensified appetites.

During conversation Rod detailed his life to Matt and Bill.

"Many folks think I'm a bit crazy, living in my cave. However, they are unaware of my circumstances. I am nearing seventy and the vista of life has changed. During my tenure at the university I became obsesses with biological research spending quantities of time in the field collecting specimens. I was caught in three separate thunderstorms and struck by" "lightning during each storm. The old adage that lightning never strikes the same place twice didn't work. It was a miracle I survived. This experience played heavy on me psychologically and the third strike put me in a coma for a week. When I regained cognition my brain function had diminished. I could not speak smoothly with long pauses and slow reacting to students and colleagues. It was exasperating causing severe anxiety. I thought clearly, but speech was muddled. It was embarrassing. I resigned from teaching and awarded full pension. From that point I began to plan my future. I had a desire to move away from social complexities. I spent many years restoring a house near campus, sold it as a means of escape. During my field research work I develop a deep love for the Ozarks with its beauty and solitude, haunting me in an enchanting manner. As you observe, my speech impediment dissipated and presently I feel no effects from the lightning strikes. I studied the lives of those who also experienced multiple strikes and some were affected similarly. From this study I learned certain physical composition enhances vulnerability to strikes. So, from this I conjectured if I am to live remotely I must discover a living design offering protection from strikes; thus, the cave. When dark clouds appear, the cave is my sanctuary. It's far more comfortable than typically imagined. My living space is arranged nicely, and I found an internal spring with the sweetest water you have ever tasted. The cave is warm in winter and cool in summer, and my life is joyful living at this place."

The two executives were mesmerized.

Matt: "What an interesting story. Do you have electricity in your cave?"

"Yes, I have a solar panel array and it works perfectly using a bank of storage batteries. I have a good short wave radio receiver and listen to short wave stations at night. I use propane for cooking and heat, but even on cold days I need very little heat. I built a doorway entrance. The place is invisible from the trail and I never have visitors. Fred knows approximately where it is I will invite him someday. Fred and Barbara are my only social connections."

This group enjoyed each other's company, such a fascinating mix. A couple carving out a life in these Ozarks, two high-end financial wizards and a retired hermit professor.

Fred: "Rod have you been listening to the news tracking an asteroid predicted to sweep close to the earth?"

"Yes, it's an interesting event. The latest report yesterday was it would be a near miss. They had been using radio beacons transmitted by satellite for tracking but the entire system collapsed, some kind of malfunction. Teams of astronomers are now the main tracking source using telescopes and hand calculations. They are in conflict. Some say it will pass others say it looks like it may strike. It's a large asteroid creating a bit of a worry."

ARKANSAS RESET

Matt: "I'm betting the beast will remain on a path away from our planet."

The next day the two executives were at their fishing spot and Rod stopped again.

"Hey you two, I must tell you the news on my radio is indicating the asteroid made a slight course change and the possibility of a strike has been upgraded to likely to happen status. Large cities around the world are beginning to panic and many are fleeing to isolated regions."

Matt and Bill looked at each other as fear overcame them.

Matt: "Thanks Rod, we are heading back to the lodge to call our offices."

Neither executive was able to make connection. They felt uncertain what to do, deciding on a wait and see approach.

Matt: "Fred, what is your opinion on this asteroid situation?"

"I've been watching the news closely, it's questionable, but in my heart I feel it could be the real deal."

"What are you and Barbara planning to do?"

"We are staying put, the world is a big place if the asteroid hits it could land anywhere, maybe in one of the oceans."

The night sky became bright as the asteroid breached the atmosphere descending at 50,000 miles per hour, speeding toward Earth. Tracking stations predicted impact someplace in mid-western United States. Populations in these vicinities were in a state of panic as chaos engulfed cities. Bomb shelters and underground areas were overloaded as fear dominated all thought.

Impact unleashed unimaginable horror. The explosion disturbed the New Madrid Fault triggering a massive earthquake. St Louis and the surrounding suburbs were obliterated;

nothing remained, leaving a fiery, immense crater of exploding gases and intense heat. All life was destroyed within a ten-mile radius of the crater. Forests in all directions were ablaze and the sky was filled with a heavy cloud of thick dust, covering hundreds of square miles. After impact came silence, broken by hissing gas and crackling flames emitting heat and smoke, an inferno of apocalyptic dimension.

Rod's cave shook violently; several small boulders broke loose and fell on his living area. He opened his cave's entrance and peered out. The lake was covered with heavy ash, about a third of the trees surrounding the lake were ablaze and the stench was unbearable. Hundreds of dead fish were floating on the lake's surface. The paradise transformed to a dismal place of death and horror. He immediately thought of the lodge and his friends. As he rowed through the ash-strewn water nearing the lodge he could see it had collapsed.

Large timbers blocked the lodge entrance, compressed by the fallen roof. Rod called out and a weak voice answered from under the debris. He then went to the utility shed and found a chainsaw and began cutting to gain access. It was Fred, he was conscious but his left leg was caught under a crumpled roof support. Rod cut the beam freeing him. Barbara was nearby moaning subconsciously with cuts on her face and arms. She was not pinned but the quake's magnitude and falling debris had caused her to become disoriented. The four had come to the lower level seeking maximum protection. Matt and Bill were lying motionless a few feet away. Rod checked Bill's pulse detecting none. Matt's pulse was weak but was unconscious. Rod then cleared a passageway through the mess of broken beams and twisted lumber. Fred had some mobility, but low strength. Rod helped Fred and Barbara to his boat, and then went back to check on Matt. He remained unconscious. Bill was dead his body had stiffened. Rod found a piece of plywood and moved Matt onto it dragging him toward the boat. With some help from Fred and Barbara they managed to get Matt into the boat and Rod began rowing toward his cave.

Through great effort they dragged Matt's unconscious body into the cave. The cave's spring was still flowing and Rod applied cold water to Matt's face and neck. He was barely breathing. After about an hour of continuous applications of cold cloths Matt's eyes opened and his breathing intensified.

"What happened? The last thing I remember is we were on the lower floor of the lodge.

Rod: "The asteroid struck dead on St. Louis, we are located just south of the Missouri border near the New Madrid Fault, and the strike triggered a powerful earthquake, destroying the lodge. St. Louis is in total ruin, no lives spared. I'm picking up short wave broadcasts from California keeping an update on conditions. This could be the world's worst natural disaster. Your friend Bill is dead, he had no pulse, and I will return tomorrow and bury him. I am so sorry you lost your friend. Fred and Barbara survived. I think they will be fine after a few days rest. I have plenty of food and the spring is undamaged. It's totally underground, no connection with the surface. Most US cities are shut down, and the government is sending troops to the vicinity of the strike to assist. No phone communication and most roads are impassable. Your car and pick up truck are crushed. We are stuck here for awhile."

The lake was absorbing much of the ash and Rod guessed some fish survived. He decided to go fishing and try to catch a few fish for dinner. He was successful, returning to the cave with four mid sized bass. He then cooked these fish serving them to his guests. Everyone was feeling relief and gratitude for being alive. Conversation centered on how their lives will unfold from this point.

"Barbara and I will rebuild, we have earthquake insurance. This kind of event is rare and the New Madrid Fault is not very active, last big quake was in the early nineteenth century."

"I must return to New York. I am worried this event will damage investments overall and I am heavily invested in commodities, which historically take a big hit when something like this occurs. Money has occupied my entire life centering my energy on the importance of money."

Rod: "When you and Bill were on the lake jigging or casting for bass did you think about money?"

"No, not a all. We kept discussing the natural beauty, and the blissful feel of being in a place offering quiet solitude and pure air. We were happy to share this time."

Rod: "I've studied and contemplated modern civilization and its many complexities. While teaching at the university I began spending more and more time in the field, couldn't get enough, becoming obsessed, immersing myself in nature and its wonder. Money is not a factor within the balanced life structure of the natural world. Money was infused by humanity, disrupting rhythmic, innate purity. Money slowly expanded its power shifting values, becoming a dominating force. Modern culture views money as opening a pathway to utopia, creating a God like status. However, it is the single most influence for corruption, provoking evil deeds, displaying possessiveness," "causing insecurity and imbalance and social disarray. We all need money during this era of human development. I need it, every month I get a check deposited in my account, but living as I do, in this cave, I am firmly attached to the Earth. I often go months on end without a withdrawal. It causes me anxiety knowing I must use money for various purposes; although, I could do without, but I too am brainwashed into thinking I really need it."

Matt: "Its so ingrained into global society we fall victim to its power, influencing us in every manner of living. Urban living is more attached to money. The entire spectrum of city life is directly connected and dependent on the power of money."

The four survivors holed up in Rod's cave for nearly a month. Finally a National Guard platoon showed up, bringing food and medical supplies. Fred and Barbara began mentally piecing their lives back together planning to rebuild. Rod stayed the same, fishing almost every day and continuing his hobby of nature study.

Upon return to New York City Matt's job was intact but he lost a significant amount of his net worth as stocks plummeted because of the disaster. Matt was feeling despair, the loss of Bill combining with the noise, clutter and polluted air of the city. He kept thinking about Rod's words, and remembering the feelings he shared with Bill on the lake while fishing together. His job was entrenched in the power of money, dissipating values located outside the realm of society's on-going quest for wealth.

Fred and Barbara bought a camper to live in while their new lodge was constructed. Rod visited them almost every day. He didn't show up for several days and Fred went to his cave to check on him. Rod had died in his sleep of an unknown cause. Fred called Matt and he visited to attend Rod's funeral. Fred, Barbara and Matt enjoyed a fine meal honoring Rod's life and their memories of him, discussing how few ever transcend to his philosophical level, adding boundless joy living each day.

After the new lodge was operational things fell back as they were before the asteroid strike. A beautiful young couple visited, enthusiastic about fishing for bass. Fred and Barbara enjoyed them so much, very lively and fun to be with. Their names were Adam and Annette. After a days fishing they returned with a stinger full of bass.

Adam spoke to Fred: "We fished all morning without a strike. Then the strangest thing happened. An older guy came along rowing a johnboat, and gave us brightly colored jigs to use for bait. He instructed us on a technique of jig fishing and in a short time our stringer was full of bass. He was dressed oddly, corduroy clothing."

Fred laughed: "Oh, that's Matt, he lives in a cave nearby and is our best friend. We endured the asteroid strike together. I'll invite him for dinner; you two will enjoy his company. He moved here from New York City giving up a career in high finance. He describes his life now as an Arkansas Reset."

Battery Acid Wine

In 1961 while hiking along the Miramichi River in New Brunswick, Canada I came upon a small path leading up the riverbank. I decided to explore this trail. As I crested the hill above the flood plain a cabin appeared. As I approached the cabin a Red Bone hound bounded down the trail toward me, barking with tail wagging, he then turned and ran back toward the cabin. The cabin door opened and an elderly woman stepped onto the porch. She waved her hand and said: "Hello, I haven't seen anyone in a very long time, come in. I'll make some tea."

    I was surprised to see her. A small woman, but hardy looking; it was apparent she was one of great beauty in her youth. I guessed her age to be mid 70's. She had been cutting firewood; with a large pile cut and split, ready to stack. She wore old fashion looking clothing, high-laced leather boots, flannel shirt and brown cotton pants, clothing style often seen in old photographs of people living in Canada in the 1920's. Her conversation revealed a quick mind. I was awestruck by this woman, living alone in the deep woods. Her dog's name was Ranger; he pushed the screen door open with his nose, went inside and plopped down in the middle of the floor. As we entered the cabin I noticed six old auto batteries stacked in a corner of the porch next to a wooden bucket with a lid. The woman's name was Laura and she told me she had lived alone in her cabin for twenty years since her husband died, her son lives in the nearby village, visits and brings supplies once a month. He tries to convince her to move to the village but she refuses to leave her cabin.

It was delightful to sit with Laura and Ranger sipping tea. During our conversation I asked Laura: "What are those old auto batteries used for?"

She laughed loudly; "Oh, those are for making battery acid wine."

"Battery acid wine?"

"It's not wine you drink, I make it for my animal friends, they come from all over, to smell it."

Laura then explained how she and her late husband enjoyed seeing the woodland animals and they developed the wine to attract them.

"I crush fruit my son brings from the village, gather certain ingredients from the forest, pine cones, wild flowers and various roots, marinate this mix in my oak bucket with battery acid. In early evening I place the bucket near the edge of the forest, remove the lid and wild critters come near the cabin to smell the wine."

"Do you do this every night?"

"Oh yes, every night."

I set my camp near the cabin and joined Laura and Ranger that evening on the porch of their cabin. We sat quietly with Ranger between us sipping our tea. In a short time movement appeared in the surrounding trees, a buck deer, followed by a snowshoe hare, a black bear, beaver, squirrels, porcupine, chipmunks, ermine and a pair of Canada jays surrounding the cabin, a surrealistic event. Laura looked at me and smiled, her eyes sparkling, as we three enjoyed this moment. I watched in disbelief, told Laura that this was the most amazing thing I had ever seen. She smiled and as darkness descended led me into the cabin and served soup and biscuits, which were surely made by God. I told her I would stop in the morning on my way out to say goodbye.

After breaking camp I approached the cabin. Laura was sawing firewood, she looked like and angel with her infectious smile. I told Laura that I would remember her forever and hoped someday to return and visit.

"You are always welcome, Ranger and I enjoyed your company."

Years passed. In 1970 I returned to New Brunswick. I was eager to find the river trail and visit with my friends. As I crested the hill I saw only an open space where the cabin was before. In its place were two wooden crosses, a large one and a smaller one. The large cross-said; "Laura", the small cross-said; "Ranger". Tears flowed.

With deep sadness I walked to the village. As I approached the village an attractive middle-aged woman was tending her garden. I stopped to talk with her.

"I visited here in 1961, hiked the river trail discovering an elderly woman, Laura, and her dog Ranger, living in a cabin near the river. Laura and her late husband had developed a concoction of natural ingredients that they marinated with battery acid and used this to attract woodland animals in the evening. Do you know anything about what happened to them?"

The woman was oddly silent, then said:

"What year did you say you visited Laura?"

"1961"

Again she became silent, but for a longer time, then sat on the ground dropping her hoe.

"Laura McKenzie was my great aunt, and as a child I would sit for hours with Laura watching the beautiful animals emerge from the forest in the evening as we sipped tea."

For the third time she became silent, then said:

"How old are you?"

"Thirty".

Now tears were flowing down her face burying her head in her hands sobbing uncontrollably. I tried to comfort her she was trembling. After a time she raised her head and said to me:

"Laura and Ranger died in a fire that burned their cabin to the ground in 1945."

We both fell silent. I hugged her, and silently walked away. I never returned to New Brunswick. Haunting memoires remain of that evening with Laura, Ranger and the battery acid wine.

Finding Level

My name is Howard Woodward. I have lived in this city for twenty years have a good paying job and live in an up scale apartment. During formative years I dreamed of city life, an ever-busy place with bright lights and ceaseless activity forming a cast of social classes mixing with urban sounds and smells. Those youthful fantasies have since waned. The city changed character; white flight caused inner city decay and crime escalated. The air is polluted from increased traffic and incessant rumble of trucks. Two blocks from my apartment is a waste incinerator spewing nightly stench. After work I visit a popular lounge as a source of tempering. Cities are connected to alcohol with consumption ranging from wandering homeless to perceived gentry.

Entering the lounge the post workday crowd fills the room, uniformly attired, posturing with prattle and exaggerated body language in an effort to conjure happiness; thus, its name "happy hour." This is a repetitious ritual tempering work place stress. As the joy juice assimilates the scene's tone amplifies. Intoxication prompts brazenness.

I amble to the bar and order a beer, sitting next to me are two beautiful women. These surroundings trigger emotions running a divided path. I am excited anticipating conversation with these women; yet, despair plagues me. Has my life become a labyrinth of mediocrity? Are values located here I don't see or understand? Do I feel happy, or am I attempting to crawl out of a rut using the brevity of the moment as a stepping-stone? Nonetheless, I am here, mingling among a smoke filled cage of interactivity.

"Hi, I am Howard, you both look ravishing."

"Thanks, I am Judy and this is Kathleen, it's our first time here. This is a busy place. Do you work nearby?"

"Yes, an accountant with a large firm, two blocks west. I live in the adjacent apartment building."

"I work close also, for a public relations company. I have known Kathleen since third grade; she seldom comes to the city. I persuaded her to visit, have some fun, dress up and experience urban life. She lives in a remote rural place, miles from the city."

"Yeah, I'm a real hick from the sticks, nice to meet you Howard. Judy portrays me as living in the jungle, foraging for food. I enjoy a city fix, maybe once a year; it's enough for me. I am having my annual beer, don't really like the stuff but feel the need to fit in. People look at you funny if you are not boozing. Judy and I were good friends growing up, were in the same high school class. She was voted homecoming queen."

"You must have been first runner up."

"Far from it. Judy lived in town with good parents in a very nice home. I lived in the country taking the bus to school. My parents died when I was very young and I stayed with my grandmother on her small homestead. During high school years my appearance was not homecoming queen material."

"It's not true Howard, Kathleen was an absolute doll in

high school. She was poor, limiting dress choices, unable to participate in the daily fashion show, but her beauty was obvious. Her personality was her greatest beauty and I enjoyed her company the most, it was so fun growing up with her, a" "laugh a minute. As you can clearly see she remains beautiful and if you know her you love her."

"Kathleen is a published writer, lives in a one hundred-year-old house inherited from her grandmother. I visit her but it's not the life for me. Her rooster wakes me up at five AM. It's still dark."

"So nice to meet you two. I readily sense character running deeper than this crowd typically offers. A writer, how fascinating."

"It's not what you may imagine. I write short stories and essays. Most have been published but the pay is atrociously low and often nonexistent. I started two novels, but could not get them to go where I thought they should and shelved them both. I do gain income from editing work of others. I have a large garden and sell organic produce at the local food co-op, also eggs. I have twenty layer hens. Defining my life, it's much work with low pay, although joyful each day. I have two dogs and three cats; they represent my social connections."

"What about me Kathleen? You e-mail me every day. I love your e mail messages, they lift my spirit."

"I take you too much for granted, but I would be a much lonelier soul without you in my life. I cannot imagine life without you. We have been connected since I can remember."

"A place in the country sounds peaceful. I am feeling intense urban burnout. This lounge is a catch basin, seeking escape, numbing brains to cope with haywire lives, work stress, money worries and a laundry list of tensions associated with unrelenting crowds of people going in different directions, it's beleaguering. An accountant's work is attached to metropolitan life. I'm stuck in this city."

The two women were startled at Howard's testimonial. The conversation stalled. Then Kathleen spoke.

"My place has its own forms of stress. Often it's difficult to make ends meet. As I awaken each morning questions appear. Can I sell enough produce and eggs this week? Will caterpillars eat my kale plants before I can soak them with organic insect spray? Will the well's pump make it through dry months? All summer I cut and stack firewood to relieve time squeeze when fall arrives. I work from dawn to dusk, never really seem to catch up. However, the air is pure and it's a quiet place, except when Ranger and Jasmine bark. Very little writing in warm months, it's mostly a winter activity."

"I am like you Howard, professionally attached to the city. Public relations firms rely on population density. I have never felt urban burnout; I enjoy the hustle, bustle atmosphere and the variety of human contacts each day. Continuous urban activity wears more on some. Lets exchange e-mail addresses, this topic is crying out for more discussion. It may lead someplace. Meanwhile, we are here to enjoy this time together. I'll have another beer."

"I'll pass, only one for me. Farmers get up too early to contend with hangovers."

"How about you Howard"

"I'll take another. I'm buying, I usually have two, sometimes three."

It felt good talking with these women, continuing through

FINDING LEVEL

a second beer and then parting ways exchanging e-mail addresses to expand thoughts later. Tomorrow is Saturday and Judy said she would drive Kathleen back to her farm planning to spend the night. Judy and Kathleen are true friends, forming a lifetime bond.

"Dear new friends: What a good feeling talking with you last night. Articulate beautiful women do a much better job relieving an old warhorse's anxieties than beer. Too much beer dissolves my memory; and brain cells are forever grateful when I stop their alcohol bath early. No hangover this morning. I'm thinking clearly, at least I think I am."

"Last month was my forty fifth birthday. Progression of time changes the tone of this annual event, diminishing celebration, forming milestones pivoting toward aging. Forty-five is a reality check, quietly stepping in cadence with timeline rhythms tipping into a zone of no return. I got married at thirty. Friends and associates were giving me a suspicious eye wondering about my late entry into matrimony. I never questioned it. I've always been a slow mover socially, and meeting someone with proper chemistry and compatibility is a consequence of luck and circumstance. Things went well for five years, and then my wife discovered greener grass cutting me loose, a difficult adjustment. It was back to work and I have been in my present routine since."

"During high school I was in a quandary about career choices, took a series of aptitude tests and accounting kept surfacing as an appropriate direction. It is fascinating how society judges us in accordance to career choices. It's as if our lives were outlined early on structuring education and ambitions toward what is socially acceptable, centering on earning money and fitting into a pattern recognized as culturally aligned, and most importantly prosperous. So, success is synonymous with money, viewing earning potential as a pathway to status, melding with conformity. This all began for me during aptitude testing in high school. Now I earn in excess of one"

"hundred thousand dollars a year leading me to where I am. I juggle numbers all day, a boring routine, then hit the lounge, suck down a few beers, and live in a high-end apartment. Is this all there is to discovering a good life?"

"Write when time allows. I look forward to your thoughts. Your new friend, Howard."

"Howard: Judy left this morning, and will probably read your message later this evening. My rooster Henry was on time forcing early rising. I marvel at his propensity for regiment. A biological alarm clock."

"Last night and also at breakfast Judy and I discussed meeting you. My life contrasts to yours and Judy's. My friendship with Judy is cemented by longevity and similar philosophical views. It's an unusual bond, sharing support, offering a sense of love and self worth. The main distinction is Judy enjoys social mingling. I like it in small doses and in recent years desire for social connection subsided. I am also forty-five, and in opposition to your thoughts I praise each day with great joy to be alive and though others may assess my life as tentative it offers intangible rewards. Money remains a factor; however, it fails to dominate. It's fun living out here. I find myself looking at the sky each day praising the sun and the life it creates. Planting kale seeds in early spring and seeing them break the soil revealing new life is difficult to describe, a personal, spiritual event."

FINDING LEVEL

"I never married, but had near misses, not quite getting there for a variety of reasons. My grandmother was an extraordinary woman. She taught me self-reliance, connecting with the soil, gaining sustenance and independence, living frugally, which is an accomplishment in itself. Work" "blends naturally manifesting from osmosis of circumstance and need. My life is untypical compared to standard employment characterization."

"My interest in literature and writing evolved from my grandmother. She was intensely literary. Read and discussed all the classic authors inspiring my writing pursuit. Also a few teachers were influential. Writing fills a void during winter months. I become impassioned with writing, softening lonely times. Winter's isolation stimulates creative thought."

"You are invited to visit any time. I suggest you accompany Judy on her next trip. She comes often; it's such joy to have her. Judy is an urbanite but feels need to embrace our unique relationship and it is apparent the beauty and quietness of this place offers renewal. These visits are comforting for us both. The most ardent isolationist needs human contact. Many consider Thoreau a hermit. This is far from truth; his life was filled with quality human connections. His cabin had three chairs and each chair was labeled with a name. Solitude, Friendship and Society."

"I sense you will benefit from visiting for a day. It's nice here. Kathleen."

"Howard: As predicted our discussion at the 'catch basin' stirred thoughts. Kathleen shared her message to you. Kathleen is right; her place does penetrate me, a profoundly alive place. I feel a certain balance when I visit, a cleansing. No question in my mind you are in need of cleansing."

"Call me 346-1181, we can plan a visit. I will drive and we can talk more on the trip to Kathleen's place. Don't attempt to evaluate her; she is the most eloquent and fascinating person you will ever meet. Talk to you soon, Judy."

"Hello Judy? This is Howard."

"Hi Howard. Glad you called. I am thinking this coming weekend would be a good time to visit Kathleen. It's late spring and she has finished planting leaving time for us. I can drive. Does this sound right for you?"

"Sure, it's exciting, an escape. Give me a time and I will be ready. My apartment is adjacent to the lounge, ring 410 and I will buzz you in."

"I will be at your apartment at 7AM, we can stop at my usual place for breakfast. I will verify things with Kathleen. She will be delighted."

"I will be ready. Lots to talk about. A break from our routines, see you Saturday."

Judy was on time ringing Howard's number. The buzzer opened the door. This is truly a luxury apartment building, in the heart of the city. Much like Judy's townhouse.

"Welcome, come in. Coffee is ready. Just one cup and then we can hit the road."

"This is a magnificent apartment."

"It's my sanctuary, where I recharge for the next day."

After coffee they were on the road to Kathleen's. A sunny, warm late spring day and Judy and Harold were comfortable with each other, both attached to urban living.

"It's about an hour's drive once we clear the city limits."

"Are you married?"

"No, I have pretty much run the gamut regarding

partnering. Never formally married but multiple relationships. Everything ranging from alcoholics to control freaks and some plagued with extreme insecurity. I tried to adjust, but as a female tending a career it was far too difficult. Kathleen has been a stalwart supporter and friend. My life always falls back to Kathleen."

"Since high school people have told me I am beautiful. Early on I bathed in this praise and attention, later realizing beauty is a double-edged sword of power and influence. It can be a curse, but also a handy device if used correctly. Opportunity linked to beauty has diminished in recent years, as aging descends."

"You are still very beautiful. You and Kathleen remain beautiful. This stimulated me to talk with you both at the 'Catch Basin'".

"We enjoyed listening to you. I think we all feel degrees of despair and anxieties within the structure of our lives. You showed sensitivity with good expression, causing feelings of attachment. This seldom happens to either of us. We are both a bit extreme with independent personalities, have an inner drive to find our own way, contrary to many women who commonly view males as elements of support."

"It sure made my day"

"Let's eat now, we are about half way to Kathleen's house."

After breakfast Judy and Howard were back on the road.

"I am eager for you to see Kathleen's farm. I think it will mellow your anxiety."

They turned off the highway onto a secondary paved road driving several miles then turning again onto a gravel road. This was a winding road through a wooded section. They came

HINTERLAND JOURNAL

to a mailbox with the name Kathleen Turner entering a one-lane dirt road. As they approached Kathleen's house two dogs came running sounding greeting barks with tails wagging. Kathleen appeared at the doorway smiling then walked into the yard to meet her friends. The dogs quieted as human petting settled them but tails continued speaking in high voice. Harold was overcome and felt grateful to have arrived.

"So glad you two came. Real people, what a treat."

Kathleen hugged them both. Her dark eyes depict her soul. One cannot help feeling this woman's grace and beauty. It is truly overwhelming and obvious.

"Come in, I want to show Howard my old house."

The house is a spacious two-story farmhouse. Built in 1910, wood siding and two chimneys. Everything was in perfect order. One corner of the large kitchen was organized to weigh and package vegetables to be sold at the local food co-op.

"This is where I live and work each day. Weekly I go to town to deliver produce and eggs. As you see, my dress choice places function above fashion. If I dressed in the city as I do daily I would be viewed with suspicion or a homeless person. It's a tough life out here, but it fits for me. I am so happy to see you two. I enjoy cooking and now I can prepare us a fine meal. I found a large bed of morel mushrooms and will combine them with dehydrated vegetables plus I started kale in late winter using my cold frame, it's ready to harvest and also have a bottle of wine."

Howard was enthralled and kept staring at Kathleen. Her hair was up, with no make up. He felt powerful emotions looking at her in her bib overalls. She was magnificent, causing him to feel awkward, thought he might stammer and stutter if he

FINDING LEVEL

spoke. Then said.

"I love your house. Judy explained a few things but seeing it offers clarity. I have never known anyone living in such a manner or capable of what you do. It impresses me. I feel energized; the beauty of the place and the quiet solitude is refreshing compared to city clutter, noise and pollution. This place has abstract splendor, an entirely different world. I am so glad you invited us to visit. It's difficult to explain, but feels good."

"I have opinions and reasons delivering me to this life. I can share those thoughts later."

Kathleen then extended the house tour showing special pride for her writing place. This was her grandmother's office also, attaching memories from Kathleen's youth. Shelves filled with books on various subjects, many gardening manuals. Her desk was orderly with published essays and short stories posted on the bulletin board above her computer desk. This is where Kathleen spends winter hours. Her writing fertilizes her soul, opening creative thoughts traveling to paper.

The three walked the property as Kathleen explained her garden. Its variety of crops and immense size seemed difficult to manage for a single gardener. Her layer hens were wandering about pecking for insects. A chicken house with wire fencing was their nocturnal space. Ranger and Jasmine slept near in their doghouse watching over the hens. Cats darted around keeping their distance, unsure about these strangers.

Kathleen prepared a wonderful meal with brown rice, chopped almonds and steaming kale with sweet onions and morels, reconstituting dehydrated peppers and tomatoes in the steamer. Topped with freshly grated ginger and crushed garlic. Seasonings included turmeric powder, fresh ground pepper and Himalayan salt with mixed organic spices. Harold had never experienced such a meal mixing healthy foods creating wonderful flavor. The wine added to the perfection.

"Now you know why I love coming here. Have you ever had a meal like this?"

"Not in my entire life. This is an unforgettable experience, combining the company of two beautiful and enjoyable women. I think I may now be in heaven."

"I am happy to share this meal with you two. It's lonely here at times, and I am grateful for the company. Food is the essence of life; it can enhance life or destroy it. Agriculture has moved in a troubling direction, becoming industrialized, relying on trickery of hybrid crops and chemicals gaining higher, faster yields using lower labor and requiring less field time. Modern food production causes widespread health issues, and agriculture is nothing like it was in earlier times. Bees are dying by the thousands, killed from ingesting chemicals attempting to pollinate. Food processing and fast food companies employ taste engineers designing foods with excess salt, chemical taste enhancers and preservatives subtracting nutritional values. I obtain great joy living as I do. I love being connected to the Earth. When large farms dwindle from drought and crops fail, my garden is saved because I can manage it. I hand water during dry times, enough to keep it thriving. Humanity has drifted far from early human balance. I feel as though I am a child of the Earth, living a dream."

Judy knew all of this, and her main intension for this visit was to expose Harold to an alternative life. His dismay may fade gaining understanding of Kathleen's philosophy of life.

FINDING LEVEL

"When I was young I envisioned city life. Cities seemed exciting, offering social encounters, the arts, libraries and exposing values toward social betterment. I enjoy brief visits to the city. My place offers a feeling of belonging, a comfort zone. I mutated to this place. The soil, the closeness to nature and blissful quiet not found in cities."

Judy, Howard and Kathleen savored this time together. The fine meal and conversations offered cohesiveness. The hominess of Kathleen's house and kitchen added an indefinable quality.

Breakfast was oatmeal, chopped walnuts with cinnamon and honey, fresh eggs and biscuits surely made by God. As Judy and Howard departed all three felt a higher bond. Howard could not escape the power of Kathleen's beauty and overall demeanor. He could not recall such feelings. Shortly after they departed Judy asked Howard.

"What are your thoughts?"

"I can't describe them. Kathleen is captivating. Her physical beauty adds to her magnetism but is a minor player to her overall being. She displays personal evolution quite above anyone I have ever known."

"As I told you."

Howard's mind kept flashing images of Kathleen in her bib overalls darting around the kitchen, stirring and chopping things, like a ballet. He thought about her simplistic, independent life, her garden, animals, and writing. These thoughts lingered forming a haunting but loving and pleasing emotion. He must now return to the noisy clutter of the city with polluted air, pulling him back into despair.

"Howard, this is Judy. Kathleen called she is in the hospital.

She was using the chainsaw cutting a small log on the ground and a large stick under the leaves was thrown back hitting her on the lower shin. It swelled badly, she didn't go for treatment immediately and the leg became infected. They put her on an IV with strong antibiotics but the doctors are worried the" "infection may spread into her bloodstream. This is a very serious condition. Kathleen is distraught worrying about her animals. I am calling you from California, I am over my head with client meetings and I can't get there quickly. I am hoping you can help out."

"Give me Kathleen's number. I will call her. She can give me instructions and I will feed and care for her animals. I will stay at her place until she recovers. I have over a month's vacation time coming."

"Her cell number is 714-866-9214. Thank you so much Howard. Call me as soon as you get there."

"Kathleen, this is Howard. Judy called and told me of your crisis. I am leaving now for your place. I will feed your animals and watch over things until you return home. Give me instructions."

"Bless you Howard. I am so worried. They have access to water, automatically flowing into a tank. The foods are in the storage shed. Feed the chickens at night, one bowl each day for the cats and dogs. It's quite simple. The house is not locked and there is plenty of food. We can talk daily until I get out of this place. The doctors are really worried, but my body is strong and I am betting on myself to recover."

"Don't worry, I can handle it. Judy is in California or she would be here, you know that."

"Hello Judy? This is Howard, I am at Kathleen's and she

FINDING LEVEL

gave me instructions to feed her animals. I will remain here as long as I am needed."

"Thank God. I am so grateful and relieved. I will come as soon as I can. I am so hoping Kathleen can recover quickly."

In one week Kathleen's leg swelling reduced and the doctor's released her prescribing oral antibiotics to continue treatment for another week. She drove her old pick-up truck home. Howard was sitting on the porch with Ranger, Jasmine and two cats on the steps. Tears formed in Kathleen's eyes. She was completely overcome with emotion.

"Howard, how can I ever thank you enough? I am going to prepare you the best meal you have ever eaten. It's impossible for me to describe the joy I felt when you offered to watch over things during my recovery."

She hugged Howard, squeezing him tight.

"I enjoyed being here at your place. It's so wonderful, addictive."

Kathleen made coffee and continued talking about her nightmare experience at the hospital while preparing food. Howard sat staring at her as she gracefully moved about the kitchen. The meal was divine as the two relished this time together. Kathleen began cleanup, putting dishes in the sink.

"Kathleen, your place is a paradise. I suffer living in the city, imprisoned, and the past week I felt I escaped prison. You are the most magnificent woman I have ever known. I feel a depth of love for you I thought did not exist. All my life I have felt off center, out of balance. While watching over your place it was as if my blurred life came into focus. When I am with you at this peaceful place I feel as if I have found level. I want to live here with you. What do you think?"

Kathleen dropped her big stirring spoon on the floor. Picked it up quickly putting it in the sink. She was silent, with one hand on the counter, staring intently at Howard with her dark, penetrating eyes. The silence was uncomfortably long, calculating response.

"I never thought of it like 'finding level', it's a wonderful simile. Are you sure you want to give up your high paying job to hoe corn and pick tomatoes? This house is a bit cold in mid winter."

"To be with you I can endure anything."

"When I write I crave solitude."

"I want to write too. Often thought about writing. We can compliment each other."

"I feel love for you too. At this juncture of our lives partnering could offer unique opportunity. I feel joyful thinking of how it could be. Bonding with this place requires a particular mentality; living remotely attaching to physical work, but rewards appears in unsuspecting places. It's like combining ingredients preparing a flavorful meal, permeation occurs, fusing with nature in its many forms. The morning rattle of the woodpecker, the haunting call of the sand hill cranes in their annual migration, the ever loquacious crows mixing with the natural smell of clean, fresh air. This place touches perfection, opening a gateway to life unfamiliar to many. Let's give it a try. Find level together. Level is good."

As Judy arrived at Kathleen's house Howard and Kathleen greeted her as she exited the car.

"OK, you two. I'm reading something on your faces, but unsure what I am reading."

Kathleen spoke: "We have good news."

Goat Power

The year is 1923 and the country has been euphoric since the end of The Great War. Alcohol flows like water fueling an era of drink, dance and celebration. Enterprise gains traction adding momentum to the industrial revolution. Manufacturing is on an upward spike with millions being made bootlegging liquor from Canada. Prohibition opens a floodgate for crime and corruption.

Nestled on a hillside high in the Catskills is a spectacular mansion. This is the home of Cyrus Wingate, a multi millionaire, his wife Margaret and their daughter Sybil. Parked on the circle drive is a Bentley limousine with three gardeners nearby performing landscaping tasks and the chauffeur is polishing the Bentley. This spacious mansion is surrounded by five hundred acres of wooded property creating a massive estate.

Wingate dabbles in a variety of business ventures, owns one third of a bootlegging operation running three schooners from Canada weekly. He ceases this endeavor, conjecturing it too risky when government enforcement escalated. He shifts to commodities and stocks, investing heavily in manufacturing and real estate. Cyrus is a large man, smokes Cuban cigars, is fifty-two years old with a swagger, has a personal tailor and uses a diamond-studded cane defining success. His wife

HINTERLAND JOURNAL

Margaret is socially connected with the rich and famous. Sybil is thirteen and privately tutored. Her teacher Dorothy is an exceptional woman, designing curriculum including academics, music, art and nature with leisure times walking in surrounding forests.

Discussions often occur at Wingate the dinner table.

"I have five hundred acres of property and every direction I view falls on land I own, with one exception, that old farmhouse on the hillside. It is owned by an elderly brother and sister inherited from their parents. They are Quakers, raise goats and that place diminishes this estate's status and value. I instructed my lawyer to contact them offering three times the property's worth. They refused the offer. It disgusts me to look at that old house each day."

"Daddy, I know those people. Dorothy and I visit with them. They are the nicest people I ever met. They are fraternal twins; their names are Dennis and Denise. They only own twenty acres and have thirty goats. They sell goat's milk and feta cheese at the local market. They were born and raised at their house, neither married and their small homestead centers their life. They talk funny, use thy, thee and thou, and dress the same every day."

"I don't care how they talk or dress, I want them and their house out of view. They are a distraction blocking my intensions and goals. This country is moving forward with higher definition of importance and worth. Two old fogies milking goats are misfits, living in the past. Money is now the power. Money pays for your tutor; it brings fulfillment and opportunity paving the road to the future. I intend to visit myself tomorrow and present a higher offer."

GOAT POWER

The next day Cyrus walked up the hillside to the old farmhouse.

"Hello, I am Cyrus Wingate. I own the mansion below. I would like to discuss purchasing your property."

"Very nice to meet thee Cyrus. It's kind of thee to visit. I am Dennis and this is my sister Denise. We have admired thy home for years. We raise" "goats; they are unique animals. Goats are hearty and endure winter better than" "cows or horses. They provide us with income to sustain our lifestyle. We also plant a large garden each year."

"My lawyer talked with you a few weeks ago concerning purchasing your land and home."

"Yes, we remember him. His offer was extraordinary, we were unaware our home and property had such high value."

"I am very interested in purchasing your property in an effort to expand my land holdings. I am prepared to offer you seventy five thousand dollars, probably four times its appraised value."

"Mr. Wingate, we cannot sell our property at any price. We are fixtures here, we have no place else to go or desire to leave. We are sixty five, and when we die this property will be inherited by our Quaker brethren and may be sold by them if they wish."

"With seventy five thousand dollars you can purchase a better place, increasing personal net worth, which can also be valuable to your Quaker brethren when you die."

"Yes, so true, observing from monetary logic. It is a vast sum of money. Our chosen living style has family roots spanning four generations. We feel obligated to live out our lives at this place and financial gain means nothing to us. Each day is a spiritual experience, knowing we are extracting sustenance from the land of our ancestors. We are extremely content and joyful to be living and working at this place."

"All right Dennis, it's beyond my understanding. Here is my card. If you change your mind let me know."

During dinner Cyrus described his encounter with the Quaker goat herders.

"I can't imagine living in such a manner, feeding and milking goats, cleaning manure, and dealing with all that for miniscule income. I would rather be in prison. Money is the impetus of modern life. Compare our lives to the Quakers. We are surrounded by luxury, and don't perform physical tasks. I make money using my brain, calculating deals and investing based on intelligent judgment. Selling canisters of milk and blocks of cheese for a pittance is a foolish and ridiculous way to earn money."

Margaret: "Well, my dear, I doubt the Quakers have your know-how, and your work is far above their comprehension. Social separation has been a presence forever. The duck tastes divine. Do you think the Quakers have ever eaten such a fine meal?"

Sybil said, "Daddy, I love those two. It astonishes me how they perform their daily tasks, bonding with their goats. They seem joyful and full of life."

"That's because you are child, and yet to learn the location of true values. Cultural structure is changing, industry and commerce are dominant, and economics rule every function of modern life. Money has power to enhance life. Thomas Edison invented the light bulb and those two still use oil lamps. What sense can that possibly make?"

GOAT POWER

"It's the way they were raised. They are accustomed to oil lamps, fitting their needs as electricity fits ours. It is what they choose."

Cyrus shrugged his shoulders and went to his smoking room for a cigar and shot of bourbon. He felt accomplished regarding his financial success looking forward to coming years expanding his wealth.

Cyrus spent the next week in New York City meeting daily with his investment banker and brokers feeling confident enough to extend his financial pursuits to higher risk stocks, allowing brokers access to his cash reserves, giving authority to purchase stocks on margin. A free rein to invest at will. The brokers made several highly profitable maneuvers pleasing Cyrus greatly. His net worth was expanding.

This pattern continued for several years, stimulating Cyrus to mortgage his home and property as a means to increase speculation capital. His total stock holdings were now in excess of ten million dollars, paying dividends each quarter.

One morning Cyrus woke feeling odd, with very low energy, drained and weak. He knew something was awry and went to a local doctor. The doctor put Cyrus in a hospital, running tests, attempting to diagnose his illness. They suspected cancer but unable to pinpoint an exact location, or even if it was cancer. It could be fatigue or possibly related to heavy smoking and drinking. In a few days, after several rounds of medication to raise his energy level he felt slight improvement and went home. His ill feelings lingered, but he remained able to monitor his finances.

One of his brokers called.

"Cyrus this is Phil. Several of your stocks are beginning

to slide. This could be temporary. I felt it necessary to inform you to consider the option of selling them. The loss will be significant."

"No, stock investments naturally fluctuate I will wait it out."

"OK Cyrus, I'll keep you informed."

On Tuesday March 25, 1929 the stock market crashed. Stocks plummeted to all time lows and investors lost millions overnight. Cyrus Wingate went from a net worth of ten million dollars to less than ten thousand in one day. Without dividends it was impossible to service his extreme debt and his home and property were in jeopardy of foreclosure.

Cyrus had never felt such despair. His health continued to decline becoming so weak he could barely walk. Upon news of financial collapse his wife left him for a wealthy acquaintance she knew through high-end social connections. His home became cold and barren, and servants quit from lack of pay. Sybil was nearing college age and there was no money to finance her education.

"Oh Dorothy. What will ever become of me? I think my father may be dying and is in such a terrible emotional state. We have no place to go."

"Sybil you can live with me if your father passes."

That afternoon Dennis and Denise visited. The mansion was cold and Dennis started a fire in one of the fireplaces.

"Friend, we read of the horrible stock market crash and combining this with thou illness thee have been dealt a terrible emotional blow. Thy wife has abandoned thee leaving only thou daughter to care for thee."

"Thanks for your concern Dennis. I feel terrible, have

GOAT POWER

difficulty walking, and it appears my net worth is now almost nothing. I am plagued with fear of dying and even if I live my future is uncertain."

"Mr. Wingate, my grandmother and mother taught me many herbal cures using various plants, combining natural healing ingredients with goat's milk. Goat's milk is among the most nutritious foods in the world. Dennis and I have a spare room and we suggest thee live with us for a while, attempting" "recovery using our knowledge of herbal cures. Often these remedies are more effective than modern drug therapy. Most illnesses manifest from inflammations, gradually weakening the body's immune system. As we age we need higher nutritional fortification ingesting anti-inflammatory foods. Inflammations may be the cause of thy illness."

Cyrus felt extreme guilt, thinking how he was intent on extracting these people from their home. Sybil read them clearly; these are caring people, living in harmonious consciousness.

With Sybil and Dorothy's help Cyrus gathered a few personal belongings and moved into Dennis and Denise's spare room. It was a small room, immaculate and orderly. On the dresser was a large ceramic bowl and a pitcher filled with water for drinking and washing. Two globe oil lamps and a clothes rack, with a large window overlooking rolling hills. Also a small wood burning stove in one corner of the room and a feather bed with a down comforter. Cyrus was taken by the sensation this small room characterized, a feeling of comfort. During the night as Cyrus lay in his bed wondering if he would live or die, his mind wandered. The warmth from the small stove and the glow of the oil lamps were therapeutic overcoming him with unfamiliar emotions. This room emitted sanctity, dissipating anxiety.

Denise combined dried herbs and root powders. Ginseng, turmeric, rosemary, holy basil, barberry, sassafras, ginger and oregano oil creating a tonic, blended with green tea, instructing Cyrus to drink this four times a day. She served oatmeal made with goat milk topped with crushed almonds, walnuts, honey and cinnamon. He also drank warm goat milk several times daily. She made special goat milk creamy soup using garden greens, thyme and diced turnips. They maintained this regimen for two weeks. No alcohol or tobacco permitted. She emphasized to Cyrus the importance of rest, and to sleep as much as possible.

Within two weeks Cyrus was feeling much better. It seemed as if a miracle occurred. He had not felt so good in years. Soon he would turn sixty, his life was at a pivot point.

Cyrus salvaged a few of his holdings. He sold the Bentley and scraped together twenty five thousand dollars. He gave this entire sum to Sybil to fulfill her college ambitions. Dorothy arranged for an entrance exam at a small college and Sybil scored exceptionally high on this test. She was accepted and the college funded a partial scholarship based upon her test score performance.

Cyrus was astonished how his energy returned, feeling young again, and felt a need for purpose. He now was sharing meals with Dennis and Denise. These two enthralled him. They functioned like a precision machine. Work routines and chores consumed each day, milking, processing cheese, gardening and keeping their small homestead orderly and productive.

"Dennis I would enjoy helping with the goats in any manner I can. As I observe your and Denise's daily tasks I feel you have reached a higher plane of living. Your daily interaction with each other and your work displays symmetry, magnifying life's definition."

"Of course, we can begin today, it would be thy pleasure to share thy work with thee. I believe physical work is the foundation of happiness, offering satisfaction and contentment."

Denise: "Cyrus, thee can live with us as long as thee wants. We enjoy thy company, and feel gratified for thy recovery."

Sybil and Dorothy visited: "Daddy, what are you going to do?"

"Firstly, you were correct about Dennis and Denise, they are the most loving, kind people I have ever met, unselfish, giving in a manner that seems to bring them great joy."

"I begin college next semester, and am enjoying living with Dorothy, she has been a great influence in my life."

"Sybil you deserve this opportunity. I enjoy each day now, and have bonded with the goats. They are comical with their slit pupil eyes and each has its own personality. I am fascinated at what they eat and how they forage for graze choices other grazing animals shun; although, they won't eat May apple; somehow they know it is poisonous. Can you believe the change in me?"

"Daddy, are you going to live here forever?"

"I don't know Dennis and Denise invited me to stay as long as I want. I intend to write a book about my experiences, investing, becoming wealthy then losing everything. Now I am wealthy again, a different form of wealth. I feel compelled to document this series of changes, my illness, recovery and the entire spectrum my life's revelations. Proceeds from this book will be donated to the Quaker brethren, their philosophy of life is the reason I am alive."

Cyrus wrote his book, describing his life in detail. How money controlled him, dominating every thought. He still feels money is important, more as a social tool. Feeling if one is blessed with an abundance of money it should be used altruistically influencing those in need, directed at the betterment of society. He titled his book: <u>Goat Power</u>. It became a bestseller earning over three million dollars. This book inspired readers to write Cyrus as the press widely covered his fall from financial grace. As planned, all proceeds went to the Quaker brethren and Cyrus became a consummate goat herder, adding dimension to his life and the lives of Dennis and Denise. He was attached to one goat in particular, Annie. Annie supplied the milk during his recovery. Denise said for unknown reasons Annie's milk seemed richer. Cyrus felt pleasure in his work, feeling deep gratitude to be alive, healthy and strong, performing manual tasks.

"Modern society is snared in superficial worship of fiscal wealth. The power of money enhances ostensibility, distorting values, stimulating materialism and exploitation, cloaking ethics existing beyond corruptive and misdirected influences of money. Money is also a tool of survival within the scope of present day social design. It is important to recognize money as a means of seeking improvement, developing and expanding the human experience; however, it is equally important to quest balance avoiding over consumption and glut, discovering frugality, allowing wealth opportunity for uniform distribution. How much is enough? It's those who have enough, but not too much who are the happiest. If monetary wealth dominates thoughts, spirituality stagnates, losing ability to recognize

GOAT POWER

and embrace the wonders of simplicity. As we transit life we are exposed to a myriad of indistinct pathways, challenging decryption and gauging worth. A selected path appearing to offer rewards is often plagued with unforeseen complexities and pitfalls, becoming apparent as we venture forth. Bliss and meaning appear in unsuspecting places, seldom easily identified. Nature displays perfection and lessons abound as we observe nature's functions. The meadowlark sings its splendid song on the upper limbs of a flowering dogwood tree and the" "catbird sings its song in the thorn bush. Nature's voice varies in rhythmic tones. All equally significant, blending in a celebration of life."

"Daily I tend my goats. Goats are designed to gain the most from the least. They herd similarly to human society. On the coldest winter days they remain active, playfully butting each other. Their requirements for sustaining life are minimal; yet, their lives are meaningful, attaining a zenith of harmony. It's the power of the goat."

Cyrus Wingate: <u>Goat Power</u>

Myrna's Story

Myrna Davis was born in 1950 and raised in an American mid western town. A beautiful child genetically influenced from her mother, combining with her quick and agile mind. Myrna was chosen homecoming queen in her high school senior year, savoring the honor and attention of this exciting event. Myrna's formative years bore the hallmark of a living, Victorian valentine.

Popular males sought Myrna's company during school years with her Mother Dorothy serving as self-appointed advisor.

Myrna received a scholarship from a nearby college entering her freshman year staying at the dormitory returning home on weekends. Male attention escalated with frequent dates to campus activities. Bill Macgregor, the son of the local Chevrolet dealer made special effort to contact Myrna. Macgregor was a good looking young man also arrogant, accustomed to having his way, given a new Corvette each year from his father. Macgregor had a reputation for short-term relationships with young, beautiful women and on continual prowl seeking a new trophy for his shelf.

Myrna eventually succumbed to Macgregor's advances and a dinner date was established. Macgregor was scheduled to pick up Myrna at 7:00 PM, arriving at 7:30 without a hint of

MYRNA'S STORY

apology. Myrna's mother greeted Macgregor with a smile.

"William it is so thoughtful of you to invite Myrna to dinner."

Macgregor nodded mumbling: "nice to be here."

Myrna looked ravishing, her dark auburn hair contrasting with bright, blue eyes accenting her intense beauty.

Macgregor reserved a table at the towns most expensive and lavish restaurant. During dinner he centered conversation on himself, explaining intention of assuming ownership of his father's Chevrolet dealership when his parents retire to their Florida home. He detailed his plan to move into their mansion with ambition to expand the dealership increasing sales and profits. Myrna was unimpressed with Macgregor, his egocentric demeanor made her nauseous and uneasy, he showed no warmth or humor, never smiled or even a slight compliment directed at her.

"Well Myrna, how about us escalating our relationship a bit, moving to a more physical level?"

Myrna was silent for a moment, then said: "William Macgregor, the son of an affluent auto dealer, a member of the gentry. During our dinner date you have dominated the conversation, incessant patter revealing a quest to increase your wealth when your parents retire. So, how am I to respond to this? Am I to feel honored, on a pedestal under a spotlight, overwhelmed by my good fortune of your interest in me? Why are we here William? I want you to take me home now."

Macgregor was stunned at Myrna's reaction and at a total loss for words. Anger then appeared on his face.

"Alright you ungrateful bitch. Do you realize how many women come on to me? They line up for my attention. You are self-centered think of yourself as beautiful. You really don't do it for me."

The valet brought the Corvette around and Macgregor got in on the driver's side slamming the door. Myrna opened the passenger door and barely got inside when Macgregor screeched the tires lurching forward before Myrna was able to fasten her seat belt. He was quiet, driving like a maniac, swerving in and out of traffic, speeding over 70mph in a 40mph zone. He glanced at Myrna evaluating her degree of fear. Then it happened. A truck pulled directly in front of them, the truck driver incorrectly calculating the Corvette's speed. It was over in flash. Myrna was driven through the windshield. The ambulance and police arrived pronouncing Macgregor dead at the scene; Myrna was unconscious and bleeding profusely from deep lacerations on her face, head and neck. Myrna was taken to the nearest hospital. After hours in ICU the lacerations were stitched and her entire face bandaged leaving only space for her eyes and mouth. She remained unconscious on a respirator. It was a horrid, tragic scene.

The year is now 2010 and a small medical clinic in a Kenyan village is the focal point of the village, with an attached room serving as a classroom to teach local children. A gray haired woman with a stethoscope hanging from her neck is tending a long line of patients. Dr. Myrna Davis healed from the tragic accident, returned to college receiving a medical degree. She is the most respected person in the village. Then one day she discovered a lump in her left breast causing concern. She traveled to Nairobi and x-rays revealed a tumor. She remained hospitalized receiving radiation and chemotherapy treatments and in time her cancer was diagnosed in remission avoiding surgery. Myrna became acquainted with a few of the doctors and nurses, who all knew of her work and clinic. Myrna looked dreadful without hair and an aging, deeply scarred face, but recognition of this woman's achievements deflected superficial judgment. Dr. Davis was an iconic figure and professional respect for her was a powerful presence.

One morning while sitting on the side of her bed, worrying about her clinic and many patients Myrna was writing in a notebook. A nurse, Julia and a friend, asked her what she was writing. Myrna told Julia it is her personal journal.

"Can I read it sometime?"

"Of course" handing Julia the journal.

"It describes my early life before Africa telling of events inspiring me to commit to those entrapped in poverty. I am also documenting my life in Africa and recently my experience with cancer."

Myrna's bedside phone rang: "Hello Myrna? This is Monique; I received a call from Kalisha informing me of your cancer. I requested a two-week leave from the hospital and they graciously allowed me time off. I am at your clinic now and will begin seeing patients in the morning. Kalisha will help me organize. Please don't worry I can handle this."

"Praise God, I have been so worried. Kalisha is as qualified as any trained nurse and familiar with patient's conditions. How can I ever thank you enough, you are my savior. I love you so much. My cancer is in remission and I should be back at work before your two-week leave is up. Call me tomorrow to update me on things. I'm feeling pretty good today."

Julia thanked Myrna for allowing her to read her journal. That evening she began reading Myrna's story. <u>The Journal of Myrna Davis</u>:

"As my recovery progressed and bandage removed I could barely tolerate looking at myself in the mirror. The facial scars were horrid, and deep. My right eye muscles were damaged and the eye was stationary, adding to my disfigurement. Depression overwhelmed me and my life seemed over. Prior to the accident physical beauty was my greatest asset carrying me to better places, opening opportunities. When I finally went home my parents were loving and supportive. This seemed to help, but the anxiety was far too great to overcome and despair intensified."

"On my dresser was an envelope from New York. One of my dorm mates was a photographer; she assembled a composite of photos submitting them to a major modeling agency in New York City. The agency's response letter said they were very interested in meeting me. Of course now such a notion was out of the question. My thoughts ended in a dead zone offering no clear path forward. It was a certainty social life would come to an abrupt halt, and it did. No more fixating stares from male admirers, mostly turn away looks, and women also distanced themselves. Women are drawn to pretty women, giving comfort to be seen with a beautiful friend creating social acceptance and identity."

"I healed enough to resume classes, which was extremely difficult. I did not return to the dorm, lived at home and commuted, shunning people as much as possible. Academic pursuits became my salvation, creating meaningful purpose, allowing a small vein of life to flow forming sanctuary."

"A few weeks after resuming classes an accident, injury attorney contacted me and scheduled a meeting. The attorney was Fred Johnson. He told me William Macgregor had a long

MYRNA'S STORY

history of speeding and reckless driving and advised me to file a claim against Macgregor's estate. In his view it was a clear-cut case. I explained the modeling agency's letter and he said it would be important regarding settlement since this opportunity is now void because of my disfiguring injuries."

'I will seek a multimillion dollar settlement. Macgregor owned one third of his father's dealership, and with his tarnished driving record no jury would refuse a large settlement. This case may take two years or more to settle but should go forward.'

"I agreed to the lawsuit and returned to my study routine directed toward a medical degree. The lawsuit proceeded slowly. McGregor's father waged an expensive, drawn out battle to protect his assets. During this time period I completed my medical school curriculum receiving a medical degree then assigned to a local hospital to serve my internship. This was my best time since the accident. My hospital associates differed from my college contacts, revealing no degradation toward me because of my appearance. I was beginning to feel a sense of my old self again. My previous physical beauty seemed less important as I was immersed in caring for patients and learning hospital procedures."

"The hospital where I was serving my internship a young black woman was also serving her internship. She was an exchange student from Johannesburg, South Africa on a scholarship grant planning to return to Johannesburg after her internship where she had been offered hospital residency. Her name was Monique Destivelle her father was French. Anti-government forces killed her father when Monique was a teenager. She lived with her mother and planned to reunite upon completing her medical training. Monique and I became close friends, and I looked forward to our meetings and discussions. She was delightful to talk with, and I enjoyed her French accent. She also was fluent in several native African languages from experiences during her father's work as a diplomat. She often accompanied him to villages and towns as a child."

'Myrna, have you read about Dr. Albert Schweitzer's historic work in Africa? It's such a wonderful and amazing story, how he and his wife established a small hospital in a very remote region of Africa now called Gabon. A fourteen-day trip up the Ocooue River to access the remote village they chose to build their small hospital in spring of 1913. You must read his wonderful book <u>The Reverence of Life.</u> This book inspired me to pursue a medical career.'

"My friendship with Monique was like a gift from God, we spent all our spare time together involving deep, insightful conversations about our lives and the choices that stood before us. Monique was a brilliant woman; reading and study consumed her life. I read Schweitzer's astonishing story describing the struggles he and his wife encountered. During Schweitzer's time European influence was inundating the continent. I became captivated by the lives of this dedicated couple as they transcended barriers and challenges to establish a hospital for no reason other than to help the oppressed."

"Anguish from my disfigurement dissipated; my life now is filled with hope and meaning. I have supporting parents, a solid career goal and a wonderful friend and colleague; although, dismay remains. Industrialized, economically driven cultures are plagued with ubiquitous over consumption, socially patterned in shallowness, image portrayal, revering

MYRNA'S STORY

material wealth with godlike status, separating from the oppressed. William Macgregor types have expanded in numbers. Selfishness is dominant. Humankind's covetousness seems boundless."

"I received a call from Fred Johnson, and a settlement had been finalized."

'Myrna, Macgregor had a large life insurance policy on his son with double indemnity upon accidental death, and the court was clearly in your favor from the get go. I initially tried for a 10 million dollar settlement but was awarded 5.5 million. The judge reduced the settlement amount. My fee will be 10%; the balance will be deposited in your bank account. I am gratified assisting you, creating potential improvement and opportunity to your life. Hopefully your future will be altered in a positive manner and it has been my pleasure to represent you. I would enjoy an occasional message informing me how you are managing your life as your medical career develops.'

'Mr. Johnson I am without words, and I am very grateful for your effort and achievement. I most certainly keep will you posted regarding my venture forward in life.'

"I was eager to discuss this event with Monique. We met at her small apartment."

'Monique, settlement on the Macgregor lawsuit has finalized. I have 5 million dollars. I'm in a daze at this point.'

'Myrna this is deserved, the suffering and effort to rise above your crisis may now open wider dimension to your future, fusing with your medical skills. It is exciting to think of the possibilities. Money is the source of most corruption but also has the power of altruism.'

'I want to open a free clinic in Sub Sahara Africa, like

Schweitzer. If I am careful with the money I can build a clinic and write grant proposals for' 'operating expenses. The clinic will exhibit validity to potential benefactors. I feel it is possible, offering meaning and purpose to my life.'

'I will support you any way I can. It's within the realm of reality. It can happen. I know you can do it.'

"After our internships Monique took the Johannesburg opportunity sharing an apartment with her mother, also as a support during her Mother's aging years. I convinced her to take time and accompany me touring poverty stricken Africa to assess potential sights for my clinic. She agreed and the experience with Monique in Africa was monumental. A life-changing event."

"I had studied in depth the various regions of Africa and knew that someplace in Kenya would be my choice. Nearly 50% of Kenya's populous is mired in absolute poverty. Many villages were without educational systems or medical services. The next meal is a challenge and often not attained. Monique and I rented a car and traveled for many days to various locations in Kenya. We neither had seen nor could have imagined the degree of squalor we encountered. Children roaming streets with swollen stomachs from malnutrition, gleaning trash heaps for anything of the slightest value. One small boy kept repeating in broken English 'Pepsi, Pepsi'. He had discovered that frequently large, discarded, plastic Pepsi bottles would have a swallow or two remaining in the bottles and was ever watchful to discover this treasure. It was heart wrenching beyond description, tears formed in my eyes. As Monique and I spoke with this child, sorrow engulfed me. When I compared my ordeal to this child's day-to-day struggle I felt a deep sense

MYRNA'S STORY

of guilt that I was in such despair, consumed by self-pity. Kenya needed me and I needed Kenya."

"Monique left for Johannesburg and I concentrated effort on central Kenya about 300 kilometers south of Nairobi. Several small villages were in this region and one particular village stirred my interest, Takula. The government red tape and paper work was overwhelming. I commissioned an enabler to assist navigate bureaucratic complexities allowing land purchase. Also by owning land, building and residence my visa became permanent. Building permits of various types were required. Within two months everything was in order and I began seeking local builders. Before I left the US I contracted an architect to draft a plan of my clinic based upon research of similar clinics. Finally all was in place and construction commenced. During construction I lived in a tent on my property."

"It was indescribably emotional witnessing my dream materialize, building this small clinic bringing medical services to the lives of many in need. Villagers gathered each day observing progress. I immediately began introducing myself explaining my mission. A young early teen girl named Kalisha visited each day and spoke English well. Kalisha was tall and strikingly attractive; her bright mind was clearly evident. Kalisha became my interpreter and guide. She schooled me on the native dialect, which was an immense help. After the construction was complete the organizational phase began and Kalisha became my paid assistant, an invaluable source relating to the entire effort. The clinic was named <u>The Place of New Hope</u> opening on June 1st 1982."

"I had not anticipated the dimension of this village's need for medical services. It was an extreme awakening, also taxing to know where to begin. My building plan included a traditional school classroom attached to the main building. I would see patients until around 1 PM and the remainder of the" "day taught children basic school curriculum. This became my routine and also my passion."

"I wrote grant proposals in the evening, sending them to every source I could locate. With the evolution of the Internet this procedure became more efficient. In time responses provided enough funding to meet operational costs and basic personal needs."

"Monique married a fellow resident doctor, a Frenchman, Alain Bissonette. Over the years they have visited often and built a small house on my property planning retirement, envisioning becoming contributors in an effort to assist these beautiful people. As age descends on me such assistance is most welcome. Monique and Alain are gifted, dedicated physicians."

"Now I am fighting the invasion of cancer and am grateful to be in remission. Cancer tends to reoccur and I will do all in my power to prevent this."

Nurse Julia returned Myrna's journal the next day.

"Dr. Davis, your life has been a challenge few could imagine. I am appreciative for the opportunity to read your journal. Reading details of your life exhibits power of persistence, discovering renewal, revealing new direction and purpose. This is a compelling story. I will never forget reading of your life."

Myrna returned to the clinic and was delighted to be back at her workspace and home. She greeted Monique and Kalisha: "I feel like I escaped from prison. I am weak, but improving each day. Monique I am forever grateful for your help. Your presence erased my worries."

MYRNA'S STORY

That evening Myrna and Monique discussed their overall situation. Monique and Alain planned to retire next year, looking forward to moving permanently into their small house becoming active participants assisting in patient care. Myrna desired to expand her school and if Monique, Alain and Kalisha assumed most clinical duties it would allow Myrna to escalate her teaching ambitions.

"Monique, I must discuss something with you that has been haunting me."

"Of course, tell me."

"As I ponder my life's unfolding arriving here with you at this clinic a sensation settles in my heart and mind. Contemplating my early life, William Macgregor, the horrid experience of the accident, the money from the lawsuit, our meeting and your introducing me to Schweitzer planting a seed leading us to where we are now. These events indicate spiritual influence, abstract, yet distinctly evolutionary generating from natural occurrences. It seems impossible what we have experienced is coincidence."

"Myrna I have never believed in coincidences always felt destiny is pre ordained and our reaction to these energies embody manifestation of goals and achievements. This does emit spiritual presence as we serve the purpose and direction given us."

Epilogue: The following year Monique and Alain moved into their small house. Myrna was so very grateful as her patient count had become difficult to manage. Myrna performed some medical duties, but Monique, Alain and Kalisha carried the bulk of patient load. Myrna loved working with children, and this new support team created opportunity for greater dedication as a teacher.

HINTERLAND JOURNAL

At the present all is well at Takula village <u>The Place of New Hope</u> clinic, as this dedicated ensemble formed a bond delivering love, harmony and assistance to many in desperate need. Myrna's cancer did not return. Monique and Alain frequently express their joy living in their simple house and truly look forward to each day. Myrna sponsored Kalisha to attend advanced nurse practitioner training in Nairobi opening potential for a higher paying job. After Kalisha completed her training she returned to the village clinic telling Myrna this is where she chooses to remain. The word spread about this small clinic in a remote village in Kenya. Benefactors appeared from everywhere, and the clinic organized a food bank with increasing monetary gifts.

Myrna's was inspired from the effects of her crisis to rise above her disfigurement. When Myrna and Monique discovered a wayward child gleaning for drops of soda in discarded Pepsi bottles, their hearts were pierced, confirming promise to that child and promises to themselves activating ambition to improve the lives of those in great despair.

As in Robert Frost's elegant poem <u>Stopping By Woods On a Snowy Evening</u> states. "The woods are lovely, dark and deep but I have promises to keep and miles to go before I sleep." The caregivers at The Place of New Hope clinic also have promises to keep and miles to go before they sleep.

The voice of destiny sings in varied rhythmic tones, often off key and out of tempo, like a catbird singing in a thorn bush. Then the sky opens and darkness becomes light as clouds of doubt vanish.

"I want to open a free clinic in Sub Sahara Africa, like Schweitzer". Dr. Myrna Davis

Foxfire

Ivaloo Johnson was fifteen years old living in a high hollow in the Virginia highlands, the only child of Arlie and Isabelle Johnson. Arlie and Isabelle homesteaded this land in 1805. Then both died in the winter of 1823 from unknown causes. Ivaloo's parents were extraordinary, building their hewn log cabin. Ivaloo buried her parents side by side near the cabin and carved their names and date of death on wooden crosses she fashioned herself. She did not know their dates of birth and living so isolated had yet to tell anyone of their deaths. The nearest neighbor was twenty miles distance. Ivaloo was tall and slender appearing older than fifteen. Her parents were gardeners and Arlie hunted game for food. Arlie and Isabelle taught Ivaloo all they knew during her formative years, she learned gardening and became an expert shot, astonishing her father at her natural ability for shooting. Ivaloo was now alone and feeling anxiety, she loved her parents deeply and their absence seemed surreal as if they remained with her. The silent solitude caused worry, thinking. "What is to become of me? Will I die alone at a young age? Can I obtain enough food to survive?" Although thin, Ivaloo was solid sinew from physical work this homestead required. She was as tough as any man with a will of iron inherited from her parents.

As the spring sun warmed the soil Ivaloo spaded and hoed the garden plot preparing for seed. She had an ample supply of canned foods remaining from winter. Each day was consumed with work associated with personal survival.

Ivaloo had a deep love for animals and as she and her father killed for food her heart was laden with guilt and only able to perform this hunting task knowing it was a necessity to live. She felt spiritually bonded to animals. She decided to attempt obtaining food without killing animals.

Repetitive dreams revealed a nightly message: "Build a fire in the woods." Each night this same message appeared. It was disturbingly haunting worrying Ivaloo. Her first thoughts were this is happening because I am alone and miss my parents so much. The mind wanders in unusual ways during lonely times.

One evening as darkness descended Ivaloo ventured a few hundred yards into the surrounding woods and built a campfire. She felt compelled to do this inspired by nightly dream. She sat on a log, feeling the warmth of the fire, penetrating the chill of the early spring night. This fire offered comfort with flames spiraling into darkness. Her mother told her many of us have spirit guides and these guides may at times communicate through dreams. Ivaloo thought: "Could this be my spirit guide speaking?"

Nothing of significance occurred that night, but the joy she felt sitting on a log next to her fire was unusual, offering a feeling of companionship. Ivaloo was overcome by a calming tranquility, a joyful feel. She let the fire burn down returning to her cabin deciding to have another fire the next evening. Ivaloo was energized diminishing loneliness.

During daily routine she thought about her campfire,

anticipating the time to enjoy her fire again. She gathered firewood at sunset. As she sat near the fire she was startled by a slight noise just beyond the fire's light. Then a pair of foxes appeared, sitting next to the fire staring at Ivaloo. These foxes remained, lying down and continuing to stare. It was peculiar, causing wonder, questioning why these foxes would do this. She smiled to herself; they were so beautiful and perfect with ears straight up. Foxes are the keenest and most intelligent of the forest animals. The foxes remained for over an hour, and then one got up and yawned. The other also stood and Ivaloo felt emotional warmth, an attachment. Then the foxes ran into the dark forest.

The next day she continued thinking about her experience with the foxes. Could not make sense of this unusual encounter. Her entire life she felt a powerful love bond for animals, often observing them for hours, mesmerized at their harmonious function. Her thoughts: "This event had a telepathic feel. Were they seeking her companionship?"

The next evening as Ivaloo sat next to her fire the foxes again appeared, each carrying a kit. They placed their kits near the fire and the two kits began to play. These were the most adorable animals she had ever seen. Her heart was filled with immense happiness watching these two. The foxes remained for a while then each parent picked up a kit and went off into the forest.

The next day the foxes came to the cabin with kits following. Ivaloo was overcome with joy as the foxes established their new den under her cabin's porch. Ivaloo now has true companions. The four foxes followed Ivaloo wherever she went and each night these friends enjoyed the reverence of their campfire. There was an element of divinity to these nightly fires.

 Ivaloo harnessed the mule and took the wagon to the small town to explain to the town's minister about her parent's death also to describe her experience with the foxes. The minister said he would visit to say prayers at the gravesites, and also wanted to see the foxes. She traded ginseng and May apple root with the storekeeper in exchange for a few basic supplies. On the return to her cabin she stopped and slept for a while then continued on. It was a moonlit night and the old mule knew his way home. Ivaloo felt fulfilled knowing she had proven herself self-sufficient, had a home of comfort and four beautiful, loving companions. Her life was complete, had purposeful meaning as she connected with the Earth in a manner seldom experienced. The enigma of life progresses to a higher consciousness when detached from human social interferences. The static of human mass hinders spiritual awareness, which is more profoundly displayed within solitude and the presence of nature. This opposes collective human instinct to gravitate toward grouping, offering social interaction and a sense security. One cannot feel the meditative powers of solitude surrounded by the buzz of human activity. Ivaloo had no choice; her position was created by circumstance.

 Each day the fox parents would hunt and return to their den with food for their kits. Ivaloo continued her homestead chores as the kits followed her every step. This routine continued all summer and by fall the kits were full size and began accompanying parents on hunts.

 Years passed and generations of foxes continued using Ivaloo's porch as their den. Ivaloo was saddened when one of her foxes would die or disappear. It was difficult but those remaining, continuing to live at her homestead strengthened her spirit. Nightly campfires were now a ritual.

Ivaloo lived until age 75. Her foxes remained attached until her death in 1883. The homestead now was now a barren place but foxes continued to den at Ivaloo's cabin. Many years passed and the land Ivaloo's homestead occupied became a National Park. The cabin was still intact and a park naturalist took an interest in the cabin presenting a proposal to restore the cabin maintaining it as a visitor attraction. The naturalist was taken by the occupation of the cabin with foxes and researched the cabin's history discovering Ivaloo's story. Ivaloo's cabin was legendary among locals. Many felt it may be haunted because each early spring a campfire is seen on the hillside near the cabin and nobody is in the vicinity when this campfire appears. The next morning after the campfire burns down fox tracks can be seen surrounding the area of the fire.

The National Park Service installed a bronze placard explaining Ivaloo's life taking over the homestead at age 15 after her parents died and her intense bond with foxes. A sign posted over the doorway states: "Ivaloo's Cabin The Home of Ivaloo Johnson and Many Foxes." It became the most popular exhibit in the park. People came from great distances to visit Ivaloo's cabin. Foxes remained, becoming accustomed to visitors. As visitors approached foxes could be seen peering out between the cabin's steps. The spirit of Ivaloo was intact and many celebrate her legacy. A mysterious campfire continued to appear each spring on the hillside near the cabin.

The Technology of Nature

The year was 2020; Phil Gordon was twenty-four, raised in an upper middle class urban environment. He excelled academically achieving a degree in computer science seeking a career in technology. Tech Solutions, a prominent software-consulting firm located in Los Angeles employed Phil.

The firm's director Jim Anderson admired Phil's technological skills and they worked well together. Jim is the coordinator, communicating with customers, discussing problems and needs. Phil was the go to guy, traveling to assigned locations seeking solutions and making recommendations. One morning between jobs Jim called Phil into his office.

"Phil, I received a message from the National Weather Service, they have a remote station in interior Alaska and are experiencing complications with their satellite tracking systems, they want us to take a look and make recommendations. Are you up for this?"

"Sure, it sounds adventurous. I have never been to Alaska."

"It's November and cold weather has set in. I will have Cindy order cold weather clothing and footwear so you won't freeze to death. Arctic Air a bush plane service out of Fairbanks will fly you in."

Within a week Phil entered Arctic Air's office meeting

THE TECHNOLOGY OF NATURE

owner Horace Green who introduced him to Willie Johansson. Willie pilots flights in and out of interior Alaska, including the National Weather Stations. Willie is a veteran bush pilot knows the wilderness routes well; also native Alaskan. The plan was to leave at 9:00 AM; the weather station is located one hundred and fifty miles North East of Fairbanks, very remote, no towns or villages within one hundred miles. The station is adjacent to a small lake, well marked for bush plane landings.

It was dark and the terminal runway was well lighted for easy takeoff.

Willie set the course North East and they were on their way. The plane was a single engine Otter, a commonly used in the Alaskan bush. About an hour into the flight Willie began fiddling with the carburetor heat lever, and the engine was not running smoothly. Willie said it was probably ice in the fuel line and if they are forced to make an emergency landing on a lake down sleeping bags and a tent are in the cargo area plus emergency rations, water and assorted survival necessities. The engine began to sound worse, missing and sputtering. Willie radioed Fairbanks giving his estimated position describing the problem. Then suddenly the engine quit running and Willie started looking for a location to land the plane. Phil knew this was a bad situation, he could see panic in Willie's eyes. There was no lake in sight for landing, but Willie spotted an open area and decided to make an attempt to land. The plane came down in a controlled pattern, but then hit the ground and both skis snapped tossing the plane into the trees. Willie's head hit very hard on the windshield and Phil's seat ripped off its mounts. His leg was broken, causing intense pain. He looked forward and Willie was motionless. He checked Willie's pulse and he had no pulse. The plane was deeply imbedded in a heavily wooded area, making it difficult for a rescue plane to see, the radio was inoperable and the plane was not equipped with a locator beacon. Phil was in great pain, but felt fortunate to be alive. Phil possessed no survival skills or knowledge of the extreme difficulty surviving in such a cold, harsh environment. The temperature was below zero, and can drop much lower at night. The Alaskan bush is a foreboding, unforgiving place. Elements at this latitude are extreme and only those habitually living with these conditions learn to adjust. The situation could not have been worse, as Phil tried to gather thoughts and formulate a plan. His mind was disoriented, spinning with apprehension and fear. He wore a parka, insulated boots and mittens, and was safe from freezing too quickly; leg pain hindered ability to move and the plane was a total mess. He knew he must locate the sleeping bags and try to make a place inside the plane to sleep calculating his only hope for survival was to remain alive and wait for rescue. He located the sleeping bags, bottled water and food rations, which were minimal. He struggled to get in his sleeping bag but managed. The plane was very cold. Phil put the water bottles inside the sleeping bag to prevent freezing. The down bag was warm and if felt good to sleep.

  Several days passed. Each day Phil heard a search plane, thought of a signal fire, but his immobility forbid him, things seemed hopeless, as the location of the plane would not be easily visible from the air. He was low on food, and the water bottles were empty. He managed to crawl to the snow melting it in his mouth; he accomplished this with great difficulty. As he lay in his sleeping bag one morning, feeling very weak and

THE TECHNOLOGY OF NATURE

distraught, thinking he surely will die, he heard dogs barking in the distance, and the sound was getting louder, indicating they are moving in his direction. Phil crawled out of the plane and shouted in the direction of the barking, and appearing in the distance was a dog sled and a man moving toward him, the emotion was indescribable, feeling he had been saved from certain death. As the dog team approached the plane barking intensified, as the dogs displayed excitement. The man was bearded and elderly, dressed in a fur skin parka, mittens, pants and mukluks. As he approached the plane, a huge smile appeared on his face, and said: "Looks like you have some trouble here, I can help you out."

Phil had never felt so good in his entire life. The man said his name was Eric Brewster, and he had a cabin about ten miles east. Eric loaded Phil on the sled and headed east from the plane. They arrived at a small cabin; Eric unloaded Phil and carried him inside. Phil was astonished at the strength of this old man. Eric put Phil on a chair and re-kindled the wood stove and soon the cabin warmed. Eric looked at Phil's leg and said he felt it was more of a cracked bone than a complete break; he then made a splint from straight tree branches and lashed it on the leg for support. Eric said he would sleep on the floor near the stove so Phil could use the cot. After a hot meal of dried salmon, brown rice and beans, with coffee Phil was feeling immensely grateful to Eric.

Eric said, "The nearest village is sixty miles east, they have a radio and a landing strip, when you heal a bit more my huskies and I will take you there so you can be picked up, we can make it in a long day if the weather is good."

Phil could not stop thanking Eric, expressing appreciation

for his rescue.

"Why do you live so remote?"

"It's a complex story, but while you are healing I will fill you in the best I can."

"How could you possibly know where I was?"

Eric was silent, then said: "Do you believe in God?"

"No, never have, I think religions are myths, created to control people and responsible for much of the world's problems and unrest."

"God lead me to you in a dream, giving me directions to find you. I believe spirit guides watch over us, protecting us, it was likely your spirit guide that entered my dream."

Phil thought this old guy is whacked out from too much isolation, but it did haunt him wondering how he could ever know to go ten miles in the direction where the plane crashed.

"What do you do here all alone, are you a fur trapper?"

"Oh no, I came to the wilderness many years ago, I kill minimally for survival needs, salmon that I dry for myself and my huskies, and a few snowshoe hares, my diet mostly is rice, beans and oatmeal. I re-stock twice a year with basic needs at the village."

"What is your purpose, do you write?"

"Yes, I keep a journal, enter something each day; my purpose is to connect with the Earth in a benevolent manner living in this magnificent place. Humankind has moved away from a loving connection with our planet. Modern humans are immersed in goals driving them away from nature and God. I feel spiritually attached to this wilderness, a communion of introspection. I live with beaver, mink and deer. I know their thoughts; touch their soul with kinship. This will be difficult

THE TECHNOLOGY OF NATURE

for you to understand, you are accustomed to urban life, where clutter, noise and congestion obstruct recognition of earthly consciousness and its infinite tides."

Phil had no response, thinking this was an odd philosophy; maybe something Eric conjured up allowing him to function in extreme isolation. Phil then explained to Eric his schooling, work and attachment to technology, and his belief that continued advancement of technology paves the future of humankind. Eric listened intently, agreeing that technological advancements are important attached to human history since inception.

"It is my belief that Earth's natural functions, and our ability to understand and blend with these functions are of the greatest importance to humankind's future, because in order for our species to live harmoniously with the Earth we must respect and understand it. Proper application of human created devices can intensify knowledge of nature's purpose, preserving it; however, to exclude nature, ignoring its importance, will ultimately prove harmful. You are likely impressed and drawn to the intricacies' and challenges associated with technology, it is quite fascinating, but natural functions of our planet are much more intricate and equally fascinating. Take the common caterpillar, it has over two hundred distinct muscles surrounding its head, allowing the radical turning required to dissect a leaf, these fascinations are endless, as one studies nature."

Phil was astounded at Eric's articulate manner of expression. Eric continued:

"You see Phil, nature by its very structure is spiritual, and there is a rhythm to it, displaying ubiquitous life forms, thriving, adjusting and embracing the elaborate designs brought forth by Earth's creation and presence. Nothing humans can create comes close to the total magnificence of nature. So many examples; for instance, the Golden Plover nests in Alaska and winters in Hawaii migrating three thousand miles across open ocean, the parent birds leave first, followed later by the fledglings, and although the fledglings have never made the trip they arrive at the same location as the parents, quite a feat of navigation I should say."

Phil was stunned: "Why do you live as you do, alone is such isolation, you have no clock, no calendar or radio?"

"I have no need for these things, I gauge activities with the sun and the seasons, deepening connection with the wilderness. I have transcended to this place, my purpose is to assimilate understanding of nature's functions. My soul lives here, and it's a joyful and enlightening experience moving metaphysically."

The two men planned to depart for the village when Phil felt he had the energy to make the trip riding on the sled. In a week it was decided that Phil had healed enough for this trip. He felt an odd sense about this cabin, a sadness to leave. Eric made wonderful food from basic ingredients, rabbit stew, bread and biscuits that were superb, sharing deep conversations about the world, its history and future. These were pleasant conversations, and Eric's mind was filled with knowledge gained from a lifetime of studying Earth's evolutionary cycles.

After a long day on the trail they arrived at the village, Eric pointed to a building where Phil could radio a message to Arctic Air. The village had a good airstrip on the frozen lake. Eric helped Phil inside the building to make the call, waiting near the woodstove:

THE TECHNOLOGY OF NATURE

"The Arctic Air owner was shocked to hear from me, he had assumed the worst, thinking I died in the crash, and was saddened to hear of Willie's death. He will arrange to pick me up tomorrow. He said he was sending the helicopter with two men, and with my help they would try to locate the downed plane, extract Willie's body and return to Fairbanks."

Eric gave Phil a roughly drawn map of the Otter's crash site so the helicopter pilot would have an easier time locating the plane.

The radio was located in the small store owned by Bill Jackson, he lived in a room built on the rear of the store, he told Phil and Eric they could sleep on the floor next to the wood stove, a very kind and pleasant man, raised in the village, was the fourth generation store keeper, serving as the town leader and responsible for communication needs.

The next morning Bill made a wonderful breakfast with eggs, bacon and hot sourdough biscuits and the three men enjoyed their company. Phil explained how he felt certain he would die in the downed Otter and it seemed like a miracle that Eric showed up with his huskies, and how eternally grateful he was to Eric. Bill told them how his great grandfather founded this little store many years ago and its founding is responsible for the establishment of the village. Bill had lived his entire life in the village, spending his youth in Fairbanks during school months, living with his aunt while attending school.

Eric said he felt the need to hit the trail, and excused himself to attend his dogs and prepare to return to his cabin. He came back into the store to say goodbye, thanked Bill for such grand hospitality, told Phil how much he enjoyed their conversations and handed him a package tied with a string in brown paper told him to open it on the flight back to Fairbanks. As Eric departed the bark of the huskies caused a stir in Phil's heart, he sensed tears welling in his eyes and then quickly quelled his emotions. After Eric was gone, while he was waiting for the helicopter, he asked Bill if he knew Eric. Bill replied, "No, never seen him before in my life." Phil was startled at Bill's response; he told Bill that Eric said he restocks here twice a year, and that he lives in small cabin about sixty miles West of the village. Bill said he knew all of the cabins and their occupants within one hundred miles of the village and he knew of no such cabin sixty miles west. Phil was dumbfounded, told Bill that he stayed at Eric's cabin for over a week while he healed enough to travel. Bill asked, "Did Eric tell you his last name?"

"Yes, it is Brewster."

Bill was silent for a moment, then said:

"I remember my grandfather speaking of a Brewster living in that vicinity, years ago."

Both men were speechless, and without comment. Soon the helicopter arrived, Phil thanked Bill and then boarded the helicopter, greeting the pilot and two men assigned to assist recovering Willie's body. He showed the pilot the rough map that Eric had given him, and asked the pilot if he could try to fly in a direction that would allow him to view Eric's cabin, the pilot said he thought he could do it. Soon Eric's cabin came into view, the pilot hovered for a minute, and Phil's face went white, the cabin was a ruin, the roof had fallen in, and trees were growing out of the cabin, it was apparent that this cabin had not been occupied for many years. Phil thought of the package Eric had given him; he reached in his parka pocket and took it out, untied the string and opened the wrapping. It

THE TECHNOLOGY OF NATURE

was a book, on the cover was neatly printed:

"The Journal of Eric Brewster 1950-1990."

Phil sat in silence until they arrived at the crash site; the two men removed Willie's body. Fortunately the fuselage had protected Willie's body from predators, and was not decomposed because of the cold temperatures, and poor Willie could now have a proper burial.

Phil had his leg x-rayed in Fairbanks, and Eric was correct, it was only a cracked bone, and the hospital put on a cast and gave Phil crutches to use until his leg healed. Phil arrived at his office in a few days; greeted by an enthusiastic office staff. Jim was so happy he survived the ordeal. They were certain that Phil had perished in the crash. Phil said he wanted to return to Alaska for another attempt at the weather station. After his leg healed he returned to Alaska, solved their problems in a few days, and then returned to the office. Phil asked to take two weeks vacation, expressing his desire to travel to a few of the National Parks. He bought backpacking and camping equipment, and drove west with the intension of camping in a few of the prominent National Parks. It was a good feeling, he read Eric's entire journal inspiring him to learn and connect more with the nature.

As he drove into Yellowstone Park, he felt emotionally lifted. The scenery was breathtaking. He camped at the park's campground to get a feel for the use of his new equipment. The next day he ventured into the nature exhibit near the campground. He approached the desk where a lovely young woman sat in front of her computer. As she greeted him, he noticed she was struggling with a computer glitch.

"Having computer troubles?"

"Oh yes, some kind of malfunction that keeps blocking data I need to access."

"I may be able to help."

Quickly Phil diagnosed the problem and showed her how to re-establish her data. She was very grateful. There was instant chemistry between these two, her name was Dorothy, and was a field biologist for the park service, telling Phil she spent quantities of time in the backcountry making animal and plant studies, recording findings, also gives nature lectures for visitors to the park. Phil was smitten. He then said, "I must ask you a question?"

"Sure, how can I help?".......... "Do you believe in God?"

Ruby Red

A vast forest spans Western North Carolina, one of the largest tracts of forested land east of the Mississippi River including Pisgah and Cherokee National Forests extending into Tennessee. In the hamlet of Clear Creek, adjacent to this forest, Jonathan McLean was born July 1, 1930. Jonathan lived in a small frame house built by his father and grandfather, who gifted the family property to build their house. Jonathan's grandmother lived nearby on a five-acre homestead. Jonathan's grandfather died in 1928, after retiring from the railroad leaving his wife Edith the house and land plus a small pension from his years of service with the railroad. This was the scene of Jonathan's early life.

Jonathan was the youngest of four boys. He had carrot red hair and also afflicted with a birth defect. His left leg had not developed properly causing him to limp, unable to run. All four boys slept in the same room. Jonathan's father Hank worked at a sawmill but money was scarce because a large portion of Hank's pay went to the local moonshiner. Hank came home from work each evening with a Mason jar of the backwoods hooch to get him through the night. Daily life was repetitive; the boys were assigned chores and if not attended to properly Hank used his razor strap as a reminder.

Brothers Horace, James and Fred intimidated Jonathan because of his impairment. Jonathan found a pocketknife on the side of the road, he treasured this knife, then Horace took it from him but Jonathan re-possessed it. Horace was furious but never retrieved the knife. Jonathan fought for his rights, and even though his brothers were bigger and would win the fight they learned the gain was unworthy of the effort. Jonathan's mother Judith defended him, but yielded to Hank who dominated the family with alcohol-fueled, iron fisted rule.

As Jonathan came of age he attended elementary school. His inability to run created a target for schoolyard bullying. The bullies would push him down laughing as he struggled to regain footing. This was an everyday event. Jonathan came to hate school with a passion although a standout in the classroom, which served to intensify the bullying. Each day was pure misery.

Jonathan survived elementary school entering junior high school; his academic achievements continued but the bullying was unrelenting. One morning he told his parents that he was not going to school and if they tried to make him he would run away. Hank quickly fetched his razor strap and Jonathan told his father:

"You can beat me all you want. I am not going to school."

"You worthless piece of shit, we will see about that."

The beatings were frequent and severe until Jonathan's grandmother intervened. Edith had power over her son. He knew she accumulated some wealth, saving over the years and was counting on his inheritance. Edith told her son never to beat Jonathan again; he can live with her and she will teach him.

Edith was truly Jonathan's savior in every way possible. His daily life made a complete reversal; he could not get to sleep quickly enough anticipating the next day. Edith taught Jonathan to recognize wild ginseng plants, harvesting the roots selling them to pharmaceutical companies. His favorite chore was to hike to the ridge in mid-summer and pick a bucket of wild blueberries. This new life was like a miracle. Edith organized a study curriculum and was astonished at Jonathan's learning capacity. One day she noticed a drawing he sketched on a brown paper bag of a fern uncurling. The perfection of this drawing revealed a gift.

On Edith's next trip to town she asked the storekeeper if he could order an artist's sketchpad and a box of drawing pencils. The storekeeper said he knew where to order these items and they should arrive next week. The art supplies arrived the following Saturday and Edith presented them to Jonathan. He was delighted to receive this gift and began drawing plants he had seen in the woods. This opened new dimension to Jonathan's life. His art expanded, making a series of magnificent pencil drawings of woodland floras. Drawing became an obsession, eventually advancing to pen and ink in addition to pencil sketches.

Entering his teen years Jonathan's life was joyful, sharing abundant love with his grandmother. Blessings continued to unfold, which seemed hopeless in earlier years.

At breakfast one morning Jonathan's grandmother spoke of their life:

"Jonathan, it has been wonderful having you live with me. Sharing homestead chores and your youthful energy has rekindled my life. When your grandfather died I felt hollow as loneliness overwhelmed me. Your grandfather Joseph was truly an exceptional man; the kindest, most giving person I have ever known and I miss him deeply. It's difficult to understand your father's lacking of compassion and love, such contrast to his father."

"Limitations caused from your birth defect expose to you a major human flaw. Intimidation toward those afflicted with disabilities is commonplace in our present culture. You are gauged socially as weak but I know you are not weak. Your impairment instills strength opening diversity to your life, exemplified by your art and love of nature. Some argue that taunting reflects natural selection, citing the code of 'survival of the fittest'. The fittest emerge from a deeper, spiritual place without desire or need to injure others. Jonathan, our time together has taught us that life's far-reaching values are more vivid when each day is embraced simplistically."

The year is 1990. Susan Willoughby is a grad student at the University of North Carolina studying for her doctorate in biology. On off days she drives to the mountain region to explore and collect specimens for botanical research. The forest is an enchanting place for a student of biological sciences. She has a special interest in mosses, which are abundant throughout Appalachia.

One day, while hiking a trail following a spectacular, fast flowing creek with moss-covered rocks she encountered a man walking in the opposite direction. The man stopped directly in front of her looking coldly into her eyes:

"Hello young lady. What are you doing out here in the wilderness?"

"I am gathering plant specimens to study at the lab at UNC, where I am a grad student."

This man had a sinister look, disheveled, causing Susan discomfort.

"Would you mind if I hike with you for a while?"

"Yes I would mind. I do not know you and you are making me feel uncomfortable, and I would appreciate it if you would continue on your way."

"I think you are very sexy looking and this is no place to be uppity. You are alone in an isolated place. I suggest you be more co-operative. I think I will walk in your direction, see what you do."

Susan was now very nervous and feeling fearful of this man. Down the trail came another man, shorter with a distinct limp using a walking staff, appeared to be in his sixties stopping next to the two. It was obvious something peculiar was occurring and he knew the other man.

"What's going on here Jeb are you giving this young woman a hard time?"

"That's none of your business Red, she don't need rescued by an old coot who can barely walk. Keep on walking and try to pick up the pace."

"This man is causing me to feel very uncomfortable, making sexual comments and asking to hike with me."

"Well Jeb, up to your old tricks again, you better move along right now."

"You just try to move me old man and see what happens."

Jeb had a menacing stare, put his hand on the handle of a big knife on his belt. Red made a low whistle and from out of nowhere bounded a big German plot hound, stood next to Red snarling at Jeb. Jeb pulled his knife moving toward the hound, but this was a big, male bear hound bred to hold a bear in place. The dog jumped like a flash to one side his jaws coming down on Jeb's wrist with full force and a loud snap was heard as Jeb hit the ground screaming with pain. The hound was Kyler, he stood over Jeb growling, showing his teeth. Jeb got up quickly and ran down the trail as fast as he could.

"Hello, my name is Jonathan McLean most people call me Red, but some call me Ruby Red. Sorry you had to run into Jeb. He's a bad one, been in and out of prison his entire life."

"Thank you so much. I was quite frightened. I am Susan Willoughby a grad student and research scientist from UNC. This is such a magnificent forest for plant specimens."

"Are you parked at the trailhead?"

"Yes."

"Kyler and I will walk with you back to your car."

"I would be very appreciative. "

"Kyler is much smarter than most hounds he can sense a situation and he knew Jeb was trouble. Normally he is the most mellow dog you could imagine, sleeps on the porch of my cabin."

As Red and Kyler accompanied Susan back to the trailhead Red explained his life, telling Susan of his troubled childhood then living with his grandmother. Red's grandmother died when he was 21 bequeathing him the homestead, angering his father, but she willed her money to his parents and three brothers. He worked at the sawmill for a while, but the boss said he was too slow moving about because of his limp and fired him. He then rented the homestead and purchased a small plot of land on the edge of the Pisgah National Forest and built his cabin. He lives off income from the rental and harvesting ginseng roots. His brothers moved away and both parents died.

RUBY RED

As they neared Susan's car they passed a small offshoot trail.

"My cabin is about 100 yards up this trail. If you decide to hike in this area again stop by Kyler and I will hike with you. My grandmother taught me many wild plants and flowers. I may be of assistance to you gathering specimens."

"Why do some call you Ruby Red?"

"When I was 13 years old I roamed the hills bringing home unusual rocks. I found one that was very unusual and red, my grandmother said it was a ruby. She told me to keep it secret where I found it and rubies were very valuable. I told one of my brothers I found a ruby, he told my father, and they tried to persuade me to tell them where I found it but I wouldn't tell. Word got around and people began calling me Ruby Red."

They arrived at Susan's car and she thanked Red again for saving her from that creepy Jeb, and said she will return next Sunday and they can search for moss specimens.

The following Sunday as Susan approached Red's cabin Kyler came bounding down the trail barking a greeting with his big tail sweeping back and forth. Red was sitting on the porch and a smile appeared on his face as Susan arrived.

"How about some coffee?"

"Oh yes, I would enjoy that."

As they sat on the porch Susan noticed several shoe boxes lined next to the cabin's wall, each had a lid in place.

"What's in those boxes Red?"

"Last week Kyler and I gathered mosses in the area thought you could make use of them."

Susan was surprised and began looking inside the boxes; a different species of moss was in each box.

"This is astonishing Red. I can definitely use these for a

paper I am preparing as part of my dissertation. I am so grateful, such a thoughtful gesture."

Red then showed Susan his cabin. Inside things were in perfect order, over a hundred books on a wide range of subjects, a small table with two chairs, an icebox, kerosene lanterns, wood stove and a fold down single bed. A photo of his grandmother was on one wall with many pen and ink drawings of plants and wildflowers on the opposite wall.

"My goodness Red, your cabin is so special, I can see you are a reader. Who did the pen and ink drawings?"

"I have been drawing plants since I was a child, it's a passion I have. I also keep a journal describing living within the forest."

Susan and Red formed a bond. When Susan was able to get away for specimen hikes Red and Kyler accompanied her.

One day when Susan visited she was obviously distraught and Red questioned her emotional state.

"I am attracted to this region for reasons beyond academic pursuits. I feel a personal alliance with the forest. Present day culture is developing into glut oriented social disorder. Earth sensitive transformations are occurring ignoring consequence intensity risking irreversible environmental loss. Population expansion, mostly wealthy retirees seeking to live in this unspoiled area are inundating Western North Carolina. Land developers symbolize an infestation of vermin seizing opportunities to purchase forestland, exploiting local landowners, profiteering building expensive, luxurious homes so the wealthy can sit on their overlooking decks soaking in the vistas. A recent proposed land purchase has angered me. It involves the purchase of a 1000-acre section adjacent to the Pisgah National Forest. The patriarch of the family who owned this land has died, but before taken ill was preparing to gift his land to create a nature preserve, passing before he could implement the deed change. This section has many old growth trees and is a haven for abundant wildlife species. I have seen bear tracks in this area. Development is pushing bears further and further into the forest. Streams are in" "jeopardy, and for certain the land will be heavily logged, with roads ripped to gain access. A few of the university's staff and prominent local citizens have formed a committee to explore options seeking to allow this land to become a preserve as was originally intended. The heirs are driven solely by fiscal gain; and it's apparent the land will go to the highest biding developer."

"Red, the committee has appointed me to meet with the family, a brother, sister and their lawyer to discuss the situation. It was decided I should go alone and calmly discuss options intending not to overwhelm this meeting. I would like you to attend this meeting with me, offering input based on your understanding the dire necessity for natural preservation."

The meeting took place at the law office of Walter Huffington, but the heirs were not present. Huffington explained they lived in Pennsylvania and asked him to convey results emerging from this meeting.

"Mr. Huffington, it is impossible to effectively persuade the heirs to consider our proposal if they are not present."

"Ms Willoughby this situation has already progressed. I am willing to listen to your presentation but must advise you concerning its relevance. A prominent land developer has offered my clients two million dollars in a single payment for the purchase of this land, although this is not absolute. I have advised them to allow ample time for additional developers to come forward with bids."

"Are the heirs cognizant of the environmental destruction developing this land will create?"

"They are aware their father's intension was to gift this land to the Nature's Conservancy and this issue was discussed; however, neither share their father's passion for preservation. They are quite materialistic with aspirations to own homes on the mountainside capturing the splendor of the valley."

Red said, "What time limit is in place before the decision is finalized?"

"Realistically 90 days would be a maximum. We have contacted several major developers highlighting this area's appeal for luxury home development. I am available to you and your committee if you are prepared to counter the current offer. Perhaps you can locate a philanthropic source to escalate the present bid."

Susan and Red departed the law office disappointed.

Huffington called his clients:

"Hello Joe, this is Walter. I concluded my meeting with the tree huggers. I don't think they have a dime; the woman is a dreamer and the old guy with her looks like a genetic mistake. Nothing's going to come of this that I can see."

"OK Walter, we want to clear this up soon, no more than 90 days. Any counter offers come in?"

"No, nothing so far."

Susan said, "Well Red it looks pretty hopeless. I will present to the committee what transpired, but the idea of a philanthropist is a pretty slim."

"Tomorrow is Sunday, good weather predicted, come up we can discuss this conundrum more thoroughly. I have a new section to show you."

It was a magnificent spring day. May apple were opening, mixing with a carpet of wildflowers creating a spiritual tonic alleviating anguishing thoughts of bulldozers knocking down trees destroying the mosaic of a majestic wilderness. Humanity's covetousness seems boundless. Habitat will be eradicated, dens destroyed driven by greed manifested by the vanity of wealth. Susan felt a sense of relief as she hiked the trail to Red's cabin hearing Kyler's familiar bark bounding toward her. Such wonder living in this place. The volume is turned down here, but the quiet is clearly audible. Sighting an owl's silent flight seeking roost in subdued morning light. The woodpecker's rhythmic beat, blending with the caw of a distant crow. This is a place of nature, a coalescence of life functioning within its own design displaying infinite splendor, a cosmic place.

"Hey Susan, glad you made it, what a grand day this is. A spectacle of new life emerging."

"So Red, where is this new area you want to show me?"

"It's not far, but we must climb a bit."

The two departed in a different direction than previous treks. About 20 minutes down this trail Red turned off the trail heading up a steep hill. No obvious trail just up the wooded hillside.

"This is a tough climb Red hope it's worth the effort."

About half way up the hill Red stopped, moved a large brushy windfall aside exposing a small cave opening.

"OK Susan, now we must do a bit of crawling."

Red took a flashlight from his pocket and the two crawled into the small cave opening. The cave opened up quickly and they could stand. Red located and lit a kerosene lantern. Susan followed Red deeper into the cave and they came to a rock basin someone had obviously built covered with small tree branches. Red removed the branches and Susan was shocked to see the entire basin was filled to the brim with rubies.

"I've been mining rubies for years. I'm certain there are several million dollars worth of rubies here."

Susan was speechless.

"This is the cave I found my first ruby when I was 13 years old, and my grandmother told me to keep it secret. You are the only other person that knows this mine exists. I have never sold a single ruby, accumulating them thinking someday they would serve a purpose. My grandmother was a spiritual person; she believed that events occur for unknown, mysterious reasons. My birth defect and struggles as a child, eventually living with my grandmother, building my cabin and moving to the mountains has led to the day we met on the trail and had to contend with that fool Jeb. Now we are given opportunity to save a threatened wilderness"

"from exploitation and destruction. I am gifting these rubies to form a foundation, which you will become the chief executive and director organizing the purchase of that precious property."

Susan became dizzy, felt faint and weak. She sat in silence for a few minutes on a nearby rock trying to absorb this experience.

"Red this is so amazing. I am lost for words."

"The first challenge is to locate a reputable jewel appraiser to learn exactly what we have. How and where to market these rubies allowing negotiation with the heirs."

"Red, I need to gather myself. I cannot think clearly, but this is certainly a miracle of some form. Let's go back to the cabin, have some coffee and think this through. Formulate a plan, discuss priorities."

"OK, good idea, but first I must express to you my thoughts. During my lifetime I have been judged negatively, with the exception of the years with my grandmother. She loved me dearly. I would have surely died without her. All human interaction toward me after her death has been degradation based upon my appearance and impairment, especially during these later years of life. The exception has been your bonding with me; it felt like the first warm day of spring, fresh and joyful. You say this discovery is a miracle; you are my miracle, allowing me to share this good fortune to save a treasured land. It is a miracle we share. This will work, the heirs, lawyer and the bidding developer worship money."

Again Susan felt weak, unable to speak, sitting quietly, taking a drink from her canteen, staring at Red, grasping for words, searching for a manner to respond. Nothing appeared. She put her hands over her face sobbing quietly, trying desperately to control herself. Such emotions are untypical of her demeanor. She had no control. Red sat quietly. After a few minutes, they walked toward the cave opening, crawled out the passage, covered the entrance and began walking in the direction of the cabin. As they neared the cabin Kyler greeted them with his welcoming bark and the three friends entered the cabin. Red put the coffee pot on.

The next day Susan was on the computer searching for jewel appraisers, located one in Knoxville, Tennessee and called. He asked her to bring a few samples and he could estimate dollar value. She drove to Knoxville and the appraiser was impressed at the quality of the rubies. Red and Susan then counted the rubies estimating their value the best they could, gauging size and purity based upon Susan's Internet research and discussion with the appraiser. Their estimate was between 5 and 6 million dollars. The next step was to sell the rubies for the highest dollar amount. Susan searched the Internet for jewel brokers. Now pieces were in place to begin negotiations with the heirs and their lawyer.

"Mr. Huffington this is Susan Willoughby. Mr. McLean and I would like to meet with you again concerning the matter of the land sale."

"Oh, hello, fine. I'm open anytime after 3PM this week. The heirs are getting uneasy about the sale and are seriously considering the present offer since no new bids have come forth. Did you find a philanthropist to assist you in your effort to purchase the property?"

"Yes, we feel things can go in our favor and satisfy the heirs beyond the present bid."

"Can you be here tomorrow?"

"Yes, we will be there at 3PM."

Susan and Red entered the law office.

"Come in, glad to see you again sit down. I am eager to hear your offer."

"We have located an anonymous benefactor. We offer 2,500,000 dollars to purchase the 1000-acre property. We can deliver a cashier's check to you when the deed is prepared for transfer. The deed should be made out to *The Ruby Red Foundation*, of which I am the chief executive and director. We will obtain counsel" "to advise and represent us regarding clarification and legality to implement proper deed transfer."

"I will inform the heirs immediately, you can call me tomorrow and I will update you on where things stand. Thank you for coming."

Susan and Red departed.

"Hey Joe, we have a counter offer for the property, the tree hugger and the old guy returned, they found a benefactor, formed a foundation and they have offered 2 mil 5 for your land. I will call the developer and present this information to him to see if he wants to increase his bid."

"Good news Walter, I will inform my sister. Let me know right away what the developer says."

Huffington called the developer, who was angered from being outbid.

"Look Huffington, those two dragged their feet, my offer is way over a realistic price for their land. I'm strung out financially; the banks are already edgy concerning another project I have in the works. The two million I offered is out of my pocket. I am passing on this one."

So, *The Ruby Red Foundation* owned 1000 acres of pristine property adjacent to the Pisgah National Forest. There will be no bulldozers, roads or uprooted old growth trees. The bears keep their home and this will become a wilderness forever, the *Ruby Red Wildlife Sanctuary*.

Susan received her PhD and became a biology professor at UNC, bought a modest house near the campus, which also served as headquarters for *The Ruby Red Foundation*. Susan put her heart and soul into the foundation. Other universities invited her to speak about the foundation's goals. Susan visited Red less often but looked forward to each visit.

HINTERLAND JOURNAL

One sunny day as Susan walked the trail to Red's cabin she was surprised that Kyler did not greet her on the trail in his usual manner. As she approached the cabin she noticed Kyler lying on the porch. His tail thumped the floor as she walked onto the porch remaining in place. Susan thought he must be getting old, or not feeling good for some reason. She walked into the cabin and Red was on his bed. She felt a surge of fear overcome her. Red had died in his sleep. Susan completely broke down, sat at the table weeping with a depth of pain she had never experienced. The anguish was overwhelming, destroying her emotional strength, a complete meltdown deep within her soul as if her heart had been torn out. Here was a loving man that gave everything he had to life, fought demons brought forth to him, transcending it all, centering purpose on connection with his beloved mountains and the life that thrives among them. He saved a wilderness that seemed far beyond his ability, was spiritually connected to his forest, never wavering. The legacy of Ruby Red was solidly intact.

"The vistas in these mountains reach the limits of spectacle permeating beyond visual, creating benevolence. One can become completely enthralled by these mountains. Stepping on wet stones as I cross a creek my heart rejoices my good fortune to live in such a blissful place." Jonathan Maclean

Susan kept Kyler and he became her trail companion during weekly treks in the _Ruby Red Wildlife Sanctuary_. Kyler accompanied Susan when she was invited to speak. She tells the story of Red's life during her talks. She posted a website describing the foundation's goals, the sanctuary's location and an invitation to visit and hike the trails within the sanctuary. Each week she includes an excerpt from Red's journal and a few of his wild plant and flower drawings. The site inspires comments from around the world, a source of joy for Susan to read.

Red willed everything he owned to Susan. Susan had Red cremated and scattered his ashes in selected places within the sanctuary. Red's cabin became a marshaling place for student volunteer trail crews and for special meetings regarding the sanctuary's management and future, also a soul spot for Susan. A few times a year Susan visits Red's old ruby mine. Rubies are no longer mined here and the mine remains a secret. She sits on the rock where she listened to Red open his heart, reflecting on the emotion of that moment.

Most often when Susan thinks of Red she remembers that pivotal day when Red and Kyler rescued her from danger on the trail. Red's spirit lives in Susan's heart, an eternal presence.

The Blues

Gazing out the single window of my small apartment the scene is a littered alley with overturned trashcans. Two cats feud over food scraps and a homeless man sleeps in the fetal position on a sheet of cardboard, wearing a long overcoat and stocking cap. The diffused glow of streetlights accent this dismal scene. This city typifies social shift caused by white flight seeking to escape urban decay, escalating racial division as Detroit spirals into a metropolitan crisis zone. The year is 1968 and the Motor City is feeling the economic toll of foreign auto manufacturing competition. Last year a race riot destroyed a large segment of the inner city. I live near the Detroit River. My apartment is adjacent to the Riverfront Bar, where I am employed.

I graduated from Michigan State earning a degree in English but my heart was in music studied as a minor. I have been a guitar student since childhood. My Mother was black and my father was a white naval officer. My only memory of my father is a photo taken of him before I was born. I have struggled with personal balance and direction my entire life. My Mother was a beautiful, gifted blues and jazz singer financing my education and influencing my musical pursuits. She also was a drug addict dying last year from cardiac arrest triggered

THE BLUES

by an overdose of heroin. My association with her musical colleagues' inspired me to master the blues and jazz guitar becoming my passion. An English degree offers limited career scope, which is why I live and work where I do.

I am recognized as a black male; however, my light skin color blocks stereotypical ethnic identity, combining with a reticent personality yielding drift toward isolation, resulting in anxiety and despair.

The Riverfront Bar gig opens opportunity for me to play jazz and blues instrumentals on Friday and Saturday night between 9:00PM and 1:00AM, but with strings attached. I am also the cleanup guy after the bar closes. The job comes with a free apartment but the pay is atrociously low. I am paid twelve dollars a day for cleanup and seventy-five dollars each night I perform plus tips. The bar is a dive; smoked filled and mostly unsavory types frequent the place, regular customers nicknamed this bar "The Sewer" because it is located near the city's main sewer overflow dumping into the Detroit River. After a heavy rain the stench is intolerable. The bar's owner charges a fee to selected hookers gaining access to display their wares and drug activity is commonplace. I tolerate this environment because of personal joy I receive performing and am grateful when customers offer compliments. Seeing my name on the small marquee causes my heart to race. "Jason McNeil Jazz Guitarist"

In recent months it is apparent my music is attracting different and larger crowds. One night last week it was standing room only for a while. During my performance break, a beautiful blond woman and two male companions greeted me with compliments introducing themselves as Jenny and

Harold Schmidt, a brother and sister and Harold's friend Joe. Jenny lives in California and is visiting her brother. Joe recommended my music, thus their visit to "The Sewer". Jenny revealed she has been drawn to blues since childhood and that she also plays the guitar.

"Blues instrumentals are beyond my skill level but I have good voice range and sing folk music, which seems a better fit."

"I enjoy folk music also. Blues is rooted in southern, slave folk music, often sung while working in the fields. Many are unaware of blue's origin. Blues evolved extensively during the depression era escalating instrumentally. Voice and lyrics form the foundation of blues music. Instrumentalists' apply intricate licks diverting attention from the vocalist, who remains steadfastly the dominant, important figure overall within blues music genre. My Mother was an extraordinary blues singer. My performing here as a solo instrumentalist allows me a personal outlet to mix a few blues pieces with jazz. But it's a shallow portrayal of blues without a quality vocalist to accompany me, or more appropriately me to accompany the vocalist. Your compliments are greatly appreciated. As a performer recognition is the ultimate reward."

"Jason I have several thoughts to share with you. I must return to California in two days and it would be my pleasure to buy you lunch tomorrow, discuss your music, especially blues relating to my recent experience in California."

"How can I refuse? My apartment is upstairs in the adjacent building. Give me a time and I will be ready."

"I will pick you up at noon."

"I look forward to it.

Jenny is a head turner, tall and elegant with vividly

THE BLUES

penetrating blue eyes forming a natural captivation. I visualize her more as an angel than a person. She arrived promptly, driving her brother's BMW.

"You are right on time. So nice of you to offer me lunch."

"Jason, your guitar playing is extraordinary, stimulating something I must discuss with you."

Jenny was raised in Detroit and took me to a nice restaurant in an affluent suburban area, a stark contrast to the "Sewer".

"I have lived in Southern California for 10 years working various jobs and singing folk music in coffee shops and a few restaurants and lounges. For the past two years I have been performing at the Blue Moon Restaurant at Redondo Beach one night a week. The owner Maurice Jackson is a blues lover and has organized a fabulous blues quartet with a lead singer that is truly out of this world; the best I have ever heard. Maurice has a fascination with folk music, which is experiencing a revival during this decade and he allows me to perform on the quartet's night off. The quartet's vocalist Jessie Brown has become a good friend and is encouraging me to sing blues. She tells me my voice is right and my range is ideal for blues. The complication I am coping with is blues singers are traditionally black influenced from blue's ethnic foundation. If I aspire to develop my blues musical skills it is unlikely I will be successful since I don't fit the traditional blues singer's image. Jessie thinks I can rise above this and has committed to work with me to develop a personal blues style."

"Of course its true black female vocalists are dominant; although, it may not be the conundrum it appears to be. Blues original lyrics reflected strife and hardship, evoking sadness, as one can imagine the pain and suffering brought forth from human enslavement. Modern blues infuses contemporary themes, presenting lyrical narrations crossing cultural boundaries. Blues offshoot is classified as 'Rhythm and Blues', which created its own offshoot called 'Rock and Roll'. It's a fascination how blues music expands into alternative, but related forms of musical expression. I am unsure I agree that race is altogether attached to blues. I read an interview with Janis Joplin a white blues singer. Janis has ventured more into a rock and roll style but her voice is pure blues. When Janis was a teenager she listened to blues recordings, especially Odetta. She went to high school in Texas, was shunned and taunted, overweight with severe acne. She carried an Autoharp wherever she went and would sing when inspired. She said she was a misfit in high school: 'I read, I painted and I didn't hate niggers.' Janis listened endlessly to blues music. She blossomed and found her place in blues. I believe she is one of the best of this era. I have all her records. I saw her perform with the Cosmic Blues Band. If your friend Jessie thinks you can sing blues I think you should give it a try."

Jenny was silent for a moment, arranging response.

"You encourage me. Maurice and Jessie met with me prior to my visit offering assistance if I decide to pursue blues. They have many contacts in the music business. I will discuss this when I return and I will also tell them I met a very gifted blues and jazz guitarist."

I felt intense attraction to Jenny. Her beauty went beyond her model image. I gave her my phone number and she promised to call after meeting with Maurice and Jessie.

"Hello Jason? This is Jenny. I met with Maurice and Jessie. They are excited that we met and feel our meeting represents a step forward for me. Maurice is flying to Detroit in a few days especially to meet you and will stop in the Riverfront Bar to attend your performance. He's a very warm and caring, successful and runs the Blue Moon with precision. I enjoyed our"

"lunch conversation adding confidence concerning my potential as a blues vocalist. How are you doing?"

"I am overwhelmed. It will be thrilling to meet Maurice. You have created positive feelings for me too. Life can take peculiar turns, often out of the blue. In our case out of the blues."

"Call me after you meet with Maurice. My phone number is: 949-346-1174"

"I will definitely call you. I am so appreciative. You are fun to talk with."

After talking with Jenny I was like a zombie. My mind was aimlessly adrift. I've never had a close relationship with a woman, plagued with shyness, observing they are drawn to extroverted men. Jenny erased introversion. I felt warmth and comfort in her presence.

Friday night as I entered the bar for my performance a tall, well-dressed black man greeted me.

"Jason? I'm Maurice Jackson; I own and operate the Blue Moon restaurant and lounge at Redondo Beach, California. I have come to hear your performance recommended by Jenny Schmidt. Jenny sings folk music one night a week at the Blue Moon."

"Such a pleasure to meet you. I am awestruck that you would take time to visit and hear my performance"

"Please don't be. We are a close-knit group at the Blue Moon and it is impossible not to love Jenny she is pure gold and I place great value on her opinion of your talent. I will stay and listen for a while and am hoping we can talk more. My plane leaves tomorrow at four PM. I would like you to join me" "for lunch tomorrow. I have a rental car and can pick you up at whatever time is convenient."

"I can be ready at eleven."

Maurice was prompt, we chatted driving to his hotel. Maurice displayed sincerity, no braggart talk. We discussed the city's vivid decay and the sadness of racial division. We sat in a quiet corner for lunch with a view of the city. Maurice began opening his thoughts.

"Jason, you are a superb player. I consider myself an expert on blues music, but it is impossible to say who is, or was the greatest blues guitarist. Styles are conceptual, forming musical abstraction. However, you are equal to the best. Jenny has a great ear for musical greatness and I knew when she described your playing my trip to Detroit would be a worthy effort."

"I am humbled Maurice."

"Blue's pioneer W.C. Handy claimed blues was introduced to him by an itinerant street guitarist at the train station in Tutwiler, Mississippi in 1903. I have studied early blues musicians. To grade or compare these greats is impossible. Blues is characterized from an overall perspective, creatively surfacing in an array of patterns and shapes like musical snowflakes."

"Jessie and I are impressed with Jenny. Her voice and demeanor are a complete package of musical gift. Jenny feels like a square peg trying to fit into a round hole as a blues singer. Blues singers are traditionally black and as a white woman Jenny feels misplaced. I sincerely feel Jenny can accomplish blues becoming accepted and admired."

"Humanity has been plagued with disharmony since

THE BLUES

inception. Racial, religious and cultural intolerance remains. If opportunity arises to transcend prejudicial boundaries, identity and acceptance, it should be approached" "enthusiastically. Music provides a potion infusing tolerance. The 13th century Persian poet and Sufi mystic Rumi taught that music, poetry and dance expose pathways to enlightenment. In my view Jenny could not be in a better position to pursue blues and eventually I feel she will agree. My goal is to encourage Jenny to work with Jessie, gaining traction with blues, feeling her way slowly. In the meantime I offer you an opportunity. The quartet's lead guitarist Bill Wright is a long time friend and a superb musician. He's 65 now and has expressed desire to reduce weekly hours. I can offer you three days a week playing with the quartet. I will sponsor you, fly you to California, help you adjust and find suitable residence. We can move forward from this point. I can pay you 500 dollars a week. Does this offer interest you?"

Jason said, "You have seen where I live and perform, a squalid section of the city. I accept with great appreciation. Music is my life and your offer is received with graciousness."

"Jason, I believe you have a great future in music. The Blue Moon's quartet is among the best. An opportunity to play with these fine musicians will significantly enhance your repertoire."

As Maurice drove me home my head was spinning with expectation. All I could think of was to call Jenny.

"Jenny, this is Jason. It's like a miracle. Maurice has offered me a spot in the quartet to fill in for his aging lead guitar player Bill Wright. I will play three days a week for 500 dollars a week. He will fly me to California and help find me a place to live. I am in a daze."

"This is such wonderful news. I will meet you at the airport gate when you arrive. Your life is taking a new direction. You won't believe how nice it is here and the quartet at the Blue Moon is the best. It's a perfect fit."

In a few days an envelope arrived with a plane ticket and a thousand dollars in travelers checks. I quit my job without hesitation. Landing in L.A. was exhilarating with thoughts running rampant forming a joy-fear emotion. Jenny was waiting at the gate with her stunning smile. She hugged me, draining my soul. What a grand day.

"Jason I am so excited that you will be included in the quartet. Maurice found a nice studio apartment for you at Redondo, within walking distance of the Blue Moon. The apartment is partly furnished, enough to get started. Isn't this great? I can't believe it is happening."

That evening Jenny met me at the Blue Moon introducing me to the quartet. I can't recall a time in my life when I felt this good. Bill Wright, expressed appreciation to have a bit more time off. Jessie explained her interest in assisting Jenny with her blues vocal development.

"Jenny's voice is ideally suited for blues in pitch and range. Soon I will present her as our guest vocalist. We have been working on a few selected blues pieces. I am certain you will be impressed. We are looking forward to you joining us. Bill has big shoes to fill; he's been a mainstay with us for a very long time. Maurice says you are capable."

I began rehearsing with the quartet. It was such a joy to play with such quality musicians and Jessie is the heart and soul of the quartet. Jenny asked me to come that evening for her folk music performance. I would not miss it for anything. She

THE BLUES

greeted me at the bar.

"Thanks for coming Jason. I have been offered to perform at a nearby coffee shop on weekends. I also have been working hard with Jessie on my blues debut. I am very nervous over this."

"Who wouldn't be nervous? This is a major direction change, new and challenging, also an opportunity. I hope I am playing when you make your debut."

I attended Jenny's folk singing gig at the coffee shop. Watching and listening to Jenny perform was pure joy. This woman electrifies a room and her voice magnifies her beauty revealing that Maurice and Jessie have identified her correctly. Jenny is a talent with immense capacity.

I received a call from Bill Wright. "Jason, the quartet is scheduled to rehearse with Jenny for her blues debut. I feel it's appropriate for you to sit in on this. Jenny is your friend and it seems the right thing. The rehearsal is at 10AM tomorrow. Can you make it?"

"Thanks Bill. I sure can and I am most appreciative for your thoughtfulness. This is important to me. A great opportunity for Jenny and me."

The quartet met the next morning at the Blue Moon. A good feeling flowed as I greeted the quartet. Jenny was talking with Jessie and waved. Then Jessie spoke to us.

"OK guys, this is a big day for Jenny. I have been working with her on 'Go Down Sunshine' and she's got it together good. If things drift a bit I won't interrupt, keep on playing and we can make adjustments afterwards. I must say this is a milestone for me also. I am Jenny's friend and take responsibility for encouraging her to pursue blues vocals. I am so looking forward to her debut."

Maurice and Bill Wright entered taking seats at the bar. Silence fell as we did the lead in measure for "Go Down Sunshine".

Jenny's voice hit dead on time with tone and depth far greater than I remembered her folk music voice. It was astonishing, overflowing with emotion, exposing her heart. If it were not for the drummer I would have surely lost beat. I was engulfed with gratitude sharing this moment with these musician and Jenny. I glanced at Bill Wright he nodded and smiled. He knew my feelings.

When Jenny finished Jessie was in tears hugging her friend and everyone stood, clapped and cheered. Jenny put her song out there with perfection and grace, shooting arrows in our hearts. Everyone gathered at the bar in a buzz over Jenny's astounding performance knowing they had just witness greatness. Maurice was beaming with delight. Jessie asked for quiet.

"Now you know why I pressed Jenny to give blues music a try. Can you imagine the fun it will be to expose Jenny to the Blue Moon regulars? I want her to debut this coming Saturday night when we have our largest crowd. It will be a night to remember."

Bill Wright altered his days allowing me to play on Jenny's special night. I entered the Blue Moon and purposely said very little to Jenny, only telling her how incredible she looked in her black cocktail dress and hair up, assuring her that I would to give her the best accompaniment I possibly could.

The crowd filtered in filling the room with muted conversations. Jessie took the stage informing the customers that they were in for a special treat.

THE BLUES

"Ladies and gentlemen, it is with great pleasure I present to you Ms Jenny Schmidt making her blues debut as the Blue Moon's guest vocalist."

The crowd responded with polite applause.

Jenny displayed no nervousness, was calm and confident. She sang <u>Go Down Sunshine</u> giving it her all. It was a divine experience. The crowd responded with a standing ovation insisting on an encore. Jenny selected <u>Piece of My Heart</u>. I nearly fell off my chair.

The customers flocked around Jenny congratulating her with compliments coming from everywhere. As Jessie promised it was a night to remember. I couldn't get near Jenny, but she spotted me and smiled staring into my eyes. After work I slipped out without speaking to Jenny who was engaged conversing with her new fans. Tomorrow was my day off and had some deep thinking to do.

I decided to write Jenny a letter:

"Dear Jenny, my beautiful and gifted friend. What a magnificent time this is for you. It's now obvious that Maurice and Jessie possessed insight beyond what you or I could have imagined exposing feelings of enchantment, impossible to describe. Last night your performance took ownership of my spirit. I have never felt such spontaneous emotion. I am familiar with the power of music to command and dominate feelings, but never have I experienced musically aroused emotions so instinctually. Your performance intensely magnifies your beauty, extending into a deep place within, erupting, unleashing greatness, which is now firmly attached to you forever"

"My question to the world is: 'How is it possible for me to not be in love with Jenny?' So much has happened, so quickly, since that special night when we met at the Riverfront Bar. From that moment I have felt comfort in your" "presence. My feelings have grown since then to the pinnacle they are now. I feel a need to talk with you about these feelings. This may offer clarity and honesty regarding our future. I don't have high expectations, I only know I feel extreme joy and gratitude knowing you and loving you. Jason"

Jenny called after she received my letter.

"Jason, I received your letter. Meet me at the beach pavilion near your apartment at 3PM. It's important to me."

"I'll be there."

I waited in the shade of the pavilion feeling the cool breeze off the Pacific. I was not nervous or tense, never have been around Jenny.

"Hey you, thanks for the letter, it made my day. We sure have come a long way in a short time. So much to talk about."

"Thanks Jenny, so glad you came. It's so nice here, such a splendid day."

"Jason, I know I have a certain beauty, it has carried me and largely responsible for my recognition. Physical beauty has been a cultural power since the beginning of humanity. It's a blessing."

"I have had two serious relationships with men; both struggled understanding the definition of the two words, relationship and ownership. They were both unsupportive in my quest to pursue music; insecure from the attention I received. Your letter struck my heart. I also feel love for you. You are a fine musician, and I gain similar emotions when I hear you play as you do when you hear me perform. We should form a blues duo; seek gigs with the help of Maurice and Jessie. I feel right

THE BLUES

about this, we are cohesive, could be such a great team."

Numbness overcame me. No words came forth. I knew I had to respond, but was so stunned my mind locked up. I looked at Jenny in silence. A long, uncomfortable time lapsed. Jenny smiled and this always melts my heart. I had to say something.

"Do you really think we can do that?"

"Of course, you are as good as any guitarist alive. I want to pursue blues, see where it can take us. I need your support as an accompanist, friend and companion. We can make this work."

So, we became Jenny and Jason a blues duo. Maurice and Jessie were supportive. Maurice became our agent. We began as an opening act for prominent concerts. This worked well and also Maurice found selected clubs and lounges for us to perform. We eventually were overwhelmed with bookings and audiences were very responsive. Maurice convinced a record producer to cut an album of our songs. This album sold well in the US and Europe. Jenny was the center of our success, proving the power of the vocalist to occupy prominence in blues music. Her magnetism took over, as audiences often would not allow us off the stage. Maurice pushed to promote a concert in San Francisco, advertised it well and we performed our first, very own concert in a mid-sized venue. What a sensation, it was overwhelming. After our encores we retreated to backstage. An usher handed Jenny a note. She read the note; handing it to me, her face was beet red.

"Jenny and Jason: I apologize for being unable to greet you backstage, but my manager and I were forced to leave early to catch a plane to London. I must tell you I was completely taken by your performance. It is my sincere hope that we can meet soon and talk about blues. Maybe consider being guest performers at one of my concerts. Isn't blues a powerful musical expression? It's been part of my life since I was a teen. You two are magnificent. Keep up the good work. Janis Joplin."

We now share a larger apartment on Redondo Beach and each day brings challenges and opportunities. One day as I returned opening the door Jenny was on the couch crying. I was startled.

"Why are you crying?"

"Janis Joplin died last night in a motel room from a heroine overdose. She was 27 years old. I can't get her out of my mind, remembering the note she wrote to us. It's so horrible. I hate drugs with a passion."

Tears formed in my eyes, it was a terrible shock to us both.

"Drugs killed my Mother too. Substances often creep into the lives of those attached to the arts. I read of an English actor who portrayed the character Sherlock Holmes so many times he became Sherlock Holmes, could not step out of character, which ultimately destroyed him as he sought drugs as an escape. Earnest Hemingway may have been the greatest writer of this century then as he aged he lost ability to organize thoughts into stories, leading to suicide fueled by alcohol. Hemingway could not live without his writing. Artistic expressions often entrap artists. I believe music attaches itself in a similar fashion becoming covetous. It is so uplifting and enlightening to perform music and be recognized we must guard against becoming imprisoned by our artistic gifts. Jenny, our partnering and bonding offers us strength and support. Drugs and alcohol artificially block anxiety.

THE BLUES

Janis drove herself to the limit with her musical talent. Her intensity was displayed when she performed. She deposited her soul on the stage, and in between times exposed a hollow dark place, a complete contrast from performing. Emptiness and loneliness overcame her. She was thrust into a void, eagerly waiting to return to the stage. She sought escape, slipped and fell down and never got up, leaving those who loved her with pain and anguish. It's so very, very sad."

We cancelled our performance talking late into the night discussing our future and made solemn promises to never use drugs or be consumed by substances.

When I am with Jenny I am in a higher place. She stirs my every cell, blissfully touching each day. Jenny delivers me to a zone of purity and purpose.

Gazing out the large window of our apartment the view is blue sky melding with blue water as the sun lowers into the vast expanse of the Pacific. Jenny is dozing on the balcony with two cats playing at her feet. The sunset casts diffused light accenting this mood of contentment reminding me of Jenny's debut song <u>Go Down Sunshine</u>.

Pathways are amorphous, often manifesting unadulterated, escaping predictability. Direction and purpose can be elusive as some meander, wandering endlessly, searching. Others discover flecks of gold as they wash the sands of time in their pan of life.

Transformation

Chicago's government housing project was built in the mid sixties. Aging has taken its toll diminishing original intention of providing quality housing for the economically oppressed. Only one elevator is in working order and used infrequently from fear of entrapment caused by mechanical failure. No maintenance personal on the premises but a few male residents crudely perform routine repairs. Walls are covered with graffiti; hallways littered with trash, discarded clothing and furniture. It's a squalid place forming a sense of hopelessness. Few living in this project have jobs, most are welfare recipients with days occupied watching hours of mindless television and drug and alcohol use are widespread.

Martha Jamison is a single mother attempting to raise her 14-year-old son Mark in this environment. Martha is a housekeeper traveling daily by bus to an affluent suburban area working for a lawyer and his wife to maintain their luxurious, spacious home. Mark is exposed to pervasive dysfunctional peer interaction. The school Mark attends offers little educational benefit with teachers serving as wardens to maintain some sense of order and discipline resembling a prison compound more than a learning institution.

After school Mark is most vulnerable to hazards of his

TRANSFORMATION

environment. Groups of youths wander about, some play basketball on the project's court and others mingle aimlessly. Mark began collecting discarded aluminum cans as a means of making a few dollars. He had several large trash bags filled with crushed cans stored in an inconspicuous place. One day two older youths approached him.

"Hey dude, hear you have a stash of cans. How about sharing with your brothers. We can find some crack and get high together."

"No way man, I worked hard collecting those cans and I am keeping the location a secret."

"Look asshole, we will beat the shit out of you if you don't tell us where those cans are."

"I'm not telling."

The beating was severe. Mark survived making it back to the project. His eyes were swollen and he was bleeding from cuts on his face and unable to attend school for a few days. Martha was terribly distraught, wondering how she can improve her son's life. She feared he would succumb to his environment. Most young, inner city, black males drift toward crime leading to prison. This place is void of opportunity. The national economy is unstable and government programs offer little worth. For a young, black male to find positive direction and enter the work force is nearly impossible.

A week later at school Mark was called to the principles office. In the office sitting near the principle's desk was a policeman and a well-dressed young woman with a brief case. The principle asked Mark to have a seat. The young woman spoke:

"Mark, I am Susan Williams from the department of social services and child welfare. I have terrible news. Your mother had a heart attack at work, was rushed to the hospital and has died."

Mark was speechless, disoriented then began to cry, sobbing deeply with his hands over his face. Here was a child on the cusp of adulthood; his mother was his source of strength and the only meaningful person in his life.

"Mark, we are required by law to assume responsibility for your welfare. This is such a terrible shock and we share your grief. Officer Jones and I will accompany you to your apartment where you must gather personal belongings and come with us to a holding center until our department can assign you to a foster home. I will personally oversee every function in your life until you are settled in your foster home. I will drive you to and from school each day."

The school principle touched Mark's shoulder: "Son, this is your only choice. Your mother was your sole supporter and now she is gone."

The holding center was a dismal barracks type facility, only a step above prison with an armed guard occupying a desk near the entrance. Mark felt overwhelming anguish crushing his spirit. His mind flashed memories of his mother, how loving and considerate she was, her dedication to offer him the best life she possibly could. To think he would never see her again was unbearable. This dreary place escalated his anxiety. His future was dark, filled with apprehension and fear, void of love falling into an abyss of futility.

Ms Williams did as promised promptly arriving each day to drive Mark to school discussing progress locating a foster home. She told him one foster home expressed interest and they would visit this weekend to evaluate the situation.

TRANSFORMATION

The Marshals' served as foster parents for over 10 years with several children passing through their home reaching adulthood. Ms Williams entered the home making introductions and inspecting what would be Mark's assigned room. Annette Marshall was the primary figure since her husband George worked at a nearby steel mill. Annette seemed a kindly person and did most of the talking. George nodded, grunting an occasional "OK, that will work." Both were obese and frumpish; although, the house was orderly and another foster child was living at the home. Her name was Joyce and she was 12 years old. Her parents died in an auto accident and family members refused her residency. She was a very attractive young girl.

On their return drive to the holding center Ms Williams asked Mark what he thought of this home.

"My thoughts are my life has been lost. I feel empty, with no future. I have nothing since my mother died. The kids in the project will likely become drug dealers, looking forward to a life of crime and welfare checks. It doesn't matter to me what you decide."

It was decided by the welfare board to place Mark with the Marshalls'. Mark moved into his small room with no window, more of a large closet than an appropriate room for a teenager. Mark's despair escalated, he was at this place only because of money paid to the foster parents. No caring feelings present. It was nearing time for the evening meal. George Marshall postured as a dominating figure in the household. He ignored Mark totally. He spoke to his wife.

"The nigger will eat in the kitchen."

Mark was shocked; he was trapped in a racist home. Ms

Williams won't check on him for a month. Mark felt isolated, overcome with fear. That night he could not sleep wondering what would become of him, if he would die as a teenager. As he lay sleepless in his bed he heard quiet sobbing coming from Joyce's room. He listened at the door and the bed was squeaking loudly with a moaning male voice. He realized George was having sex with Joyce. He opened the door.

"What the hell are you doing? I am reporting this to the welfare agency. You are a scumbag, piece of shit."

George leaped from the bed grabbing Mark.

"Who do you think they will believe a worthless nigger or me? You report me and I will kill you. That's a promise."

Mark retreated to his small room. He was shaking and consumed by escalating fear and uncertainty. He saved 200 dollars from his can-recycling project, hidden among his belongings. He knew he had to escape this place. After the amoral, degenerate was asleep Mark crept into the kitchen filling his book pack with as much food as he could. He then exited the back door becoming a homeless waif with no plan or direction. He knew he had to leave and oddly a calming strength consumed him.

Mark's initial thought was he must leave the city. He was a fugitive from the system and his photo would be distributed among police and displayed in public places as a runaway child. He had an approximate idea of his location, calculating if he walked all night he could reach the Greyhound Bus Station. He developed a reading habit in school and during library time enjoyed reading of remote and beautiful places. He was especially attracted to the Ozark Mountains a low range running east and west in Northern Arkansas and

TRANSFORMATION

Southern Missouri. He felt necessity to relocate far away from Chicago or any other large metropolis. He would soon be fifteen and could pass for older. The plan was dubious but this was irrelevant, he felt his life was so far down the hole of despair that even a faint glow of light was most welcome. It surprised him how he was without fear or apprehension, it didn't matter what challenges were ahead, thoughts of living with that monster as a foster child was far worse than anything he could possibly encounter.

Arriving at the bus station just after daylight he studied the Greyhound routes running through Arkansas. He chose the small town of Johnsonville on the fringe of the mountains as his destination. He paid one hundred dollars for a one-way ticket and the bus would depart at 9:00AM. He had a pack full of food and one hundred dollars remaining, welcoming the opportunity to be far away from Chicago.

Mark slept on the bus arriving at Johnsonville. Johnsonville is a very small town. One grocery store and gas station combined. Post office and volunteer fire department, population seven hundred with modest houses and an elementary school. He walked to the store purchasing a quart of milk. An old pick up truck then pulled up parking in front of the store. An elderly woman emerged from the driver's seat. She smiled greeting Mark.

"Hi there, what's your name? I haven't seen you around here."

"I am Mark Jamison, just arrived on the Greyhound from Chicago and am considering relocating here. My mother died and I have no family."

"Nice to meet you Mark. I am Bernice a retired teacher

and have lived in the area for a long time. Do you want a small job today? I have been contending with arthritis and have some difficulty lifting and moving things. If you help me with my groceries and carry firewood from my woodpile into the house I will pay you ten dollars."

"Sure, I will be happy to help."

Mark felt a surge of joy meeting this elderly woman. He sensed she was one of quality and substance. They arrived at Bernice's home, a hewn log cabin far off a gravel road nestled among a grove of pine trees. Mark had never seen such a place, quite an opposite dwelling from the project in Chicago. He unloaded the groceries and then filled the wood rack inside near the stove. Bernice was an immaculate housekeeper; her cabin was orderly with several bookshelves filled with books on a variety of subjects, a desk, typewriter and filing cabinets. Bernice paid Mark ten dollars.

"How about some tea? I baked scones yesterday."

"Thanks Bernice, I am a bit hungry."

Bernice put on the teakettle, inviting Mark to take a seat at the kitchen table.

"So, are you a runaway?"

Mark was surprised she read him so clearly. He then explained in detail his life in the project, his mother's death and his horrid experience at the foster home. Bernice listened intently.

"What are your plans now that you have arrived in the Ozarks?"

"I don't know exactly what I will do or where I will go but I knew if I were to remain alive I had to escape my situation in Chicago. It was horrible and my decision was based upon no matter what happens I would find a better place. I have never

TRANSFORMATION

known anyplace except inner city Chicago. I studied various places far away from cities and was drawn to the Ozarks."

"That is quite a story Mark. My husband of forty years died last summer. We were professors at the university, retired and bought this land and cabin with ambition to embrace nature more intimately. We were both writers and felt this time of our lives offered opportunity to express thoughts on the importance of humanity re-connecting with nature as a means of discovering more peaceful social balance and direction. Your confinement in a large city and the dysfunctional human behavior you experienced exemplifies problematic social disorder inundating global society."

"I live alone and struggle with physical chores this place requires. From the description of your life to this point it's clear you cannot return to Chicago and in the meantime while you adjust you are welcome to live here. I have a spare room and I can assist you finding new direction with your life. Problems exist in the Ozarks also; many are racist and will view you with suspicion. Living with me will offer sanctuary and an opportunity to gain positive momentum forward."

Mark was in disbelief. He felt as if a miracle had descended on him. Thinking just 24 hours ago he was in as bad a place as he could be. He thought of poor Joyce trapped in that horrid place living with a person void of morals and she had no means of escape. He would write the welfare agency explaining why he ran away hoping they will investigate George Marshall and send him to prison for rape. He desperately needed Bernice, far more than she needed him. Her body is reacting to age but Mark's entire being was at risk; nearly destroyed at a very young age by social horrors he was born into. The experience of a chance meeting with Bernice had a feel of divine intervention. Destiny has lead Mark to this place.

"Thanks Bernice. I will help as much as I can. I would never imagine living in such a place. I love your cabin and feel fortunate for the opportunity. I will do my best."

"Mark, I value education and from your description of life thus far I fear you have been greatly deprived. My cabin is a place of learning. I learn each day. I study nature surrounding my home. As a teacher I can assist with your education, which is a necessary element for life's pursuits and acceptance."

Mark's life in Chicago offered no positive elements or understanding life outside his fixed environment of buildings, noise and clutter combining with a sense of fear, emotional stress and absence of contentment.

Bernice was an exceptional woman in every manner. She was an early riser filling each day with planned activities. Mark entering her life offered comfort and tapping his youthful energy allowed her to continue living at her cabin looking forward to each day, writing and observing animals and plants surrounding her beautiful residence. She became Mark's legal guardian determined to add dimension to his life as he does to hers. She homeschooled Mark, establishing a daily curriculum and he responded with enthusiasm displaying natural thirst for knowledge. Mark felt as if he had been displaced to another planet. His life in the project had no comparison to his life with Bernice. He learned to use a chainsaw cutting and hauling firewood. Bernice had a small garden and Mark was drawn to the idea of growing food and the joyful feeling attaching to the earth directly, extracting sustenance offering a feeling of independence. He went for long walks in the forest with

TRANSFORMATION

Bernice and she taught him to recognize the many varieties of plants. Explaining how ancient cultures used plants for food and medicinal use. The May apple, ginseng and sassafras offer healing powers used today in modern medicine. Mark became a dedicated gardener tutored by Bernice. He has now lived with Bernice for two years, helping with physical chores. They became intensely bonded and the joy of living in such a natural place erased memories of Chicago.

One morning during breakfast Bernice expressed her thoughts.

"Mark, I struggled to understand humanity's spiraling descent from Earth's rhythms, grading itself as the dominant species, the most powerful; yet isolated from Earth's natural tides. As you described your surroundings in Chicago it struck me your experience vividly displays imbalance. Those with very little or nothing are in a quagmire, as materialistic social orientation rules. How can living in such desperate conditions offer social traction when traction does not exist? Despair overpowers, giving in to the void of separation. In nature is found balance, embracing life simplistically, viewing basic needs as a position of prominence. Modern social order forms standards, assigning slots, displaying subtle supremacy as those placed higher on the communal pedestal indirectly control those entrapped in the plight of poverty. This condition has been in place for thousands of years."

"Bernice, I don't see how this will ever change. Separation continues to develop as those struggling on the low end of society founder, unable to climb to a higher position, whereas those maintaining positions of power guard against intrusion fearing loss of social dominance and influence."

"I believe change is possible through expanding consciousness, in an effort toward learning and applying knowledge. It's a matter of reestablishing social perimeters mentored by nature. In nature narcissism does not exist. Beauty abounds within the natural rhythms of life, wildflowers blossom to attract pollinators. Humanity can rise above self-imposed dysfunction, discovering social equilibrium. Russian writer Andre Chekhov said: 'One cannot escape from prison if they are unaware of being in prison.' As a modern species we are imprisoned within ourselves and recognition of this represents a beginning. Balance and harmony was prominent among early human cultures. The ancients had distinct advantage because of lower populations. Modern social design increases challenge but through more intense spiritual linking, applying less environmental intrusion, we can grow beyond our attachment to non-essential consumption and desire to dominate. Sage Mildred Norman, also known as Peace Pilgrim said: 'It's those that have enough, but not too much that are the happiest.' This is so very true."

Mark never had such a discussion or thought of humanity's missteps, accepting his fate in the project without the slightest conception of life evolving from influential cultural complexities over centuries of time. Bernice's insight recognizes disparity brought forth from a lifetime of philosophical study, revealing nature's demonstration of distinct unification within Earth's myriad of cycles.

"Mark you display exceptional academic ability. It is my plan to soon have you tested by the state education board a process home schooled children must adhere to, establishing qualification for a certified high school diploma. I

TRANSFORMATION

feel you are ready for this test. You are nearing your 18th birthday and it is my intension to sponsor you to attend the University of Arkansas when this time arrives. My husband Phil and I had no children, and I am gaining rewards I missed through guiding you and am pleased with your response. I feel you have great potential based upon our time together and much of this development is attached to your difficulties as a child in that impoverished place. Your early life struggles strengthened you."

Mark entered the University as Bernice planned. He excelled achieving a degree in biological science. The National Wildlife Institute employed him to write papers on animal and plant studies. Also writing grant proposals to fund a project designed with Bernice's assistance to educate the importance of preservation, fusing social unity with Earth's natural functions. Mark continued to live with Bernice, traveling to accommodate work demands.

Epilogue: Bernice lived to the age of 92. She willed everything to Mark including savings she and her husband accumulated. Mark never left the cabin, building a summer camp on the property inviting 20 teens each summer from inner city locations to stay at the camp for weeklong seminars offering hands on opportunities teaching the importance of earthly connections. Mark married Kathryn, a fellow biology student. Kathryn added great strength and meaning to Mark's life and purpose. This partnership was one of great love and devotion to each other and sharing goals.

Often Mark would reflect on his life. He remembered especially that fateful day when he was drinking his quart of milk and Bernice drove up in her old pick up truck. Bernice offered transformation and Mark responded. Mark and Kathryn are now on a mission to transform others to a better place and understanding, feeling rhythmic pulsations of the planet.

During Mark and Kathryn's promotional speeches they distributed printed excerpts from Bernice's journal:

"Thoreau imposed that simplicity opens opportunity for contentment discovering life's inner joys. How true this logic is, in every sense of living. The human experience has fallen adrift of simplistic elements seeking a more complex path. Some argue this new age reflects change of permanence and alternatives cannot intervene with current social direction. My debate is in opposition to this view. Civilization as we know it today formed thousands of years ago in the Mesopotamian region as cities formed and monetary systems were installed as a necessity of survival. This social structure has expanded and is solidly in place today. The power of wealth produces ability to control and manipulate; this condition will likely remain but change and improvement can evolve from the human heart and an ability as a species to rise above selfishness finding ultimate gratification within compassionate altruism."

"Lessons abound in nature. Life existing outside modern social design offers stability, longevity and an intrinsic capacity to adjust, flowing harmoniously with Earth's patterns of ever changing and challenging conditions. In nature opportunity for life to flourish is presented, embracing perfection and strength to reproduce blending with Earthly offerings."

"Humanity can emulate nature by leveling favorable elements seeking life's qualities. We should not have widespread poverty. We should not have extreme contrast in

TRANSFORMATION

educational systems. Thoreau's simplistic logic applies. Equality is not complex."

"The voice of destiny sings in varied rhythmic tones, often off key and out of tempo, like the catbird singing in a thorn bush. Then the sky opens and darkness becomes light as clouds of doubt vanish." Bernice McCarthy.

Wolf Spirit

The bush plane's skis touched down on a frozen lake in Northern Ontario; from her co-pilot's seat Amanda scanned the bleak winter landscape in the receding light. The fishing camp was closed, boarded up for winter. They taxied to the landing dock hurriedly disembarking. Veteran Canadian bush pilot Hubert Hallihan and Amanda Clark from Montana unloaded two light packs, put on snowshoes and began walking a trail leading away from the camp, Amanda moving quickly ahead in the half-light. The mile trail led to a small cabin nestled among a grove of hemlocks. The cabin door was unlocked, and within minutes Hubert started a fire in the woodstove and started the generator. Amanda took off her parka and heavy boots, the cabin was in perfect order, shelves filled with books and canned goods with an ample supply of firewood stacked near the stove. Hubert began preparing food. Amanda sat at the desk and turned on the computer, she immediately began opening files and searching titles, then found what she was looking for; Morris Jamison's Journal.

"My first entry comes with ease: The world is going sour. Cultural division sweeps a wide swath with its sword of intolerance. I am recording these thoughts as 2020 begins and my bones are telling me I am 65 approaching longevity's wrath."

WOLF SPIRIT

"Technological advances have come quickly, indiscriminately gratuitous, failing to project influences, hastening to implement self serving functions resulting in rampant exploitation creating loss of moral direction and diluting ethics. Global society is in contraction."

"During salad days youth energy drove me, work became my master finding success as it is socially recognized. Obsessive fiscal quest obscured spiritual awareness and I now feel despair recognizing this misdirection. My mind wanders, searching for enlightenment, seeking higher meaning and purpose."

"During my business career I vacationed with coworkers in Canada at a remote fly in fishing camp. We visited this camp over a period of years becoming friends with the Canadian family operating the camp. During these trips I felt transformed, refreshed, as if someone opened a window in a stale room. The beauty and solitude of the North Country opened introspection, vanishing when I returned to work. Thoughts of this beautiful place continued to haunt me."

"I remembered a cabin located about a mile from the main lodge, thought it may offer stimulation to awaken my spirit living at this cabin, absorbing the magnificence of the forest, seeking sanctuary from ubiquitous social decomposition. I discussed my plan with the Canadians, they said the cabin needed work but was in good condition overall and they had no objection to me occupying the cabin, emphasizing winter would be challenging; although, ski plane service is available,"

"only a few months are without air service, during freeze up and again during break up, until water is clear to land float planes. The Canadians knew my deep love for the North Country and were aware my decision regarding this venture would not be considered without careful thought and planning. I will install a portable generator, connect my computer to satellite service and also have a satellite phone for emergency use. I have several close e-mail correspondents softening lonely times."

"I drove to Port Loring, Ontario, chartered a bush plane to access the fishing camp to discuss details of my plan with the Canadians. I wanted to inspect the cabin taking along assorted tools and supplies. This new course rekindled youthful energy. The plane landed on the lake arousing memories of grand times with my friends. The splendor of the area is breathtaking, a sense of purity. My Canadian friends welcomed me preparing a fabulous perch dinner, with my plans centering conversation. They offered a room at the lodge; I stayed one night but was eager to visit the cabin, determined to stay at the cabin regardless of its condition, evaluating improvement needs of my new home."

"I hiked to the cabin the next morning and was pleasantly surprised. The roof and chinking needed work, but the stove and flue were in good condition. I spent the next few days improving and organizing, hired a young man from the lodge to help cut and stack firewood. From his knowledge he estimated winter's firewood" "need and by mid September things were in order. The computer and satellite phone functioned well, powered with the generator. The Canadians used a motorized hauler to carry in a fifty-gallon drum of gasoline for the generator; they also carried in my food supply. The lodge would close on October 1st, and they gave me a key in case of an emergency."

"My first cold fall evening was filled with emotion, feeling the warmth of the wood stove, preparing a meal. It was late September with a chill in the air, a harbinger of winter's fury. I felt fear/love instincts imposing cautionary enchantment. I contacted several of my closest e-mail correspondents. Amanda Clark is my most frequent writer. Amanda is a tall, athletic woman; she lives in Montana working for the National Park Service as a naturalist and field biologist. Amanda has spent many winter months in remote cabins while researching Alaskan wolf/caribou interaction and habitat, her papers on wildlife research are widely published. Amanda is a woman of great knowledge and experience connected with wilderness areas; she became my check-in person, allowing me a level of comfort. One could not have a better check-in person than Amanda."

"It is now mid December, heavy snowfall makes daily tasks of carrying firewood and getting the generator running difficult. Early one evening while reading my e-mail, there was a distinct scratching on my cabin door. I grabbed my flashlight and opened the door. Nothing in sight, but just off the porch were wolf" "tracks, no mistaking them. This is an odd occurrence. Wolves distance themselves from humans; the few I have seen quickly turn and run in opposite direction. This strange event was on my mind for days, wondering why a wolf would react in such a manner. A week passed, and then more scratching, no wolf in sight, but a dead snowshoe hare was on the porch near my door. The next day I skinned the rabbit and made rabbit stew. Again scratching, I opened the door, and just off the porch was a wolf, with penetrating eyes, fixed on mine, remaining about a minute, then turned and ran back into the dark forest. I was in disbelief."

HINTERLAND JOURNAL

"Another week passed, no scratching. I regarded the incident as a freak occurrence. Then one evening scratching returned. As I went to the porch just beneath the steps he stood. I shined my light on him but he remained stationary. This was a magnificent wolf, with very long legs, mostly white mixed with flecks of gray. He seemed more skittish than earlier. I felt cold and went back inside to get my parka, thinking he would be gone when I returned, but he remained in place. I did not know what to do – was without understanding. As I was thinking of returning to the warmth of my stove thoughts appeared as if the wolf were projecting thoughts. It was disturbing, then mellowed. 'I am Wolf Spirit and I have come as your messenger and guide.' These thoughts were distinct and clear, and then Wolf Spirit turned and ran into the forest."

"Each night Wolf Spirit appeared at my cabin projecting thoughts. Wolf Spirit told me I was chosen because of my desire to live in the home of the wolf, sharing understanding and intense love for the wilderness. Wolf Spirit said he had been reincarnated thousands of times as a wolf with his first reincarnation from human to wolf. His people were nomads, ancient tribes following mammoth herds. They were hunters, creating a natural condition for his reincarnation to a wolf, as wolves are also hunters. In time I realized that Wolf Spirit was able read my thoughts. I projected to Wolf Spirit that I decided to live at this cabin to escape social chaos. Humanity appears to be on a path of self-destruction that may also cause Earth's demise. Wolf Spirit then said: 'Earth will survive; it is too powerful to succumb to human inability to harmonize. Human decline and failings will serve as a redirection, renewal and growth, attaining an eventual zenith that will in time regain

WOLF SPIRIT

balance.' Wolf Spirit then became silent moving back into the forest, as he had done previously."

"I was dazed, without words to describe this encounter. I thought about writing Amanda. She would surely think I had lost my mind. Wolf Spirit did not visit my cabin again, but I would often see him during snowshoe treks, always at a distance. His lope was distinct; I would stop and watch him, there was fluidness to his movement, such grace and beauty, mesmerizing. How grand to be a wolf; yet harsh and challenging to hunt and survive. The average wolf's life span is eight" "years. As time passed Wolf Spirit was not seen, I worried about him, always looking for him during snowshoe treks. I researched the web to learn about the spirit of the wolf, discovering that Wolf Spirit's serve as a transitional guides for wolves and other animal incarnations. The spirit of the wolf also has connection to Sirius, the Dog Star, used by mariners as a navigational guide."

"As I listen to the nightly opus of wolves tears form in my eyes thinking of Wolf Spirit, wondering where he has gone. I am obsessed with seeing him again. I agonize, with thoughts questioning the purpose of Wolf Spirit's decision to visit my cabin, and feel a certain spiritual power to our bond. I must continue to trek and seek my beloved friend, try to find him, and connect once more."

Here the journal ends.

Epilogue: "Dear Ms Clark, corporal Fielding and I have done an extensive search for your friend Mr. Jamison. Upon arrival at the cabin we noticed snowshoe tracks leading away from the cabin. We followed these tracks for over a mile; the tracks entered a large meadow and abruptly ended. Near the

HINTERLAND JOURNAL

center of the meadow were many wolf tracks; however, no sign of blood nor was a body found. I regretfully report that we have given up the search. We request, if possible, for you to visit the cabin, examine Mr. Jamison's effects, and possibly discover a clue to the event or events that caused Mr. Jamison's disappearance. We are at your service for any possible assistance. Regards, Sgt. Andrew McNeil RCMP"

Non-Fiction

A Place to Live

Habitat forms a foundation for living. Global overview reveals habitats range from Buckingham Palace to cardboard shanties in third world countries. Some live without a place of permanence sleeping in culverts or under highway overpasses. The gentry erect walls surrounding their homes discouraging intrusion. Archeological findings disclose details describing shelters of ancient cultures contrasting with modern times. Contemporary home selection reaches beyond basic comforts becoming an ego driven quest to gain social status and identity.

Aaron Spelling, a highly successful film and television producer is an extreme example. Aaron was horribly bullied in his youth, physically abused by schoolmates, often bedridden recovering from injuries. Aaron was an intense student and reader, developed savvy for business and filmmaking yielding great success and immense wealth. He decided to build the most spectacular home possible. The result was a 56,000 square foot mansion valued at 150,000,000 dollars. This mansion is near Los Angeles where on given nights the homeless exceed ninety thousand. Such examples prompt a question. Do modern home patterns reflect social advancement or regression?

Early human habituations demonstrated simplistic, uniform social order and conformity. The Adena people existed between 1000-200 BCE occupying the area, which are now central Ohio, Pennsylvania, West Virginia, Indiana and Kentucky, near the Ohio River. This society epitomized congruity, were cohesive and communal. They were mound builders and Adena artisans carved figures in stone remaining visible along the riverbank. Their housing was especially fascinating. Round structures using poles buried in the ground in a circular shape covered with skins or bark. These homes were strong, uniform and functionally efficient. The needs of the tribal unit occupied a position of priority, disregarding social separation with an absence of dwelling vanity. Archeological theory is that the Adena created living designs for future Native American tribes. So, did the Adena know something modern society has failed to recognize?

Thoreau's cabin was one room, a fireplace, bed, table and three chairs. Each chair was given a name, solitude, companionship and society. Thoreau practiced austerity; he understood the value of one's ability to live in comfort with less.

In nature homelessness is nonexistent. All birds, mammals and insects create homes, singularly their most valuable tool for survival insuring longevity.

Baffin Island is a barren, arctic island with granite boulders and flora of mosses and grasses. Wolves have lived on Baffin Island for thousands of years forming dens among the many boulders. These wolves are classified as Arctic Wolves and do not pack like their southerly cousins the gray wolf; although, male and female hunt as a team and the only game is small rodents, arctic hare and lemmings. Their established dens recycle to the next generation and the pathways in and around the dens have grooves worn. These grooves are in solid granite giving perspective to timeline. The Baffin Island wolves sought a place of safety and comfort. Wolves

A PLACE TO LIVE

demonstrate social balance.

On my property is a hay barn, filled with bales of hay. An opossum created its home in the barn digging an access. I often see this opossum in the early PM leaving its home to scavenge for food. Opossums are prehistoric, dating from the dinosaur era. This small mammal survived and the dinosaur perished. They are among my favorite animals, champion survivors.

Nature displays an array of dwellings and it is a fascination to study these unique and creative structures. I found an abandoned sparrow's nest on the ground. I was astonished at the perfection of this nest. Horsetail hair was used for construction material. Each hair was precisely placed, forming a perfect circle. Human hands would be challenged to form this creation.

Beehives and hornet's nests are engineering marvels. High in the oak tree is a squirrel's home, lined with selected insulating materials for warmth and comfort. While hiking my property trail one early spring the ground was covered with a light snow. I came upon a pile of woodchips at the base of a tree. High on this tree was a hole created by a pileated woodpecker. The hole was on the eastern side for protection from prevailing storms.

Humanity has moved away from its natural connections with the earth. Nature clings to the tides of universal consciousness, blending and adapting to its offerings. Human society attempts to adjust its environment to suit perceived needs, exaggerating comforts, distancing from nature's simplistic lessons. Extravagance is a harbinger for social separation and dysfunction.

An Ascetic Life

In current times worldwide social and cultural activities exposes collective ingrained mentality placing economic position and social distinction in prominence creating a sense that if fame and wealth are attained all the complex pieces of life fall perfectly in place, giving forth bliss and comfort. Think about it, everything you ever wanted a finger's touch away, all the money you could possibly spend, surrounded by comforts and luxuries scaling the heights of imagination. Is it necessary to emulate royalty to discover a fulfilling and meaningful life? Are the highest points of bliss achieved via fiscal ability?

The most intelligent and happiest people I have ever known was an elderly couple I met in Belize, Central America in 1982. They lived in a cabana and owned a small plot of land on the coast near the fishing village of Placentia, scratching out a modest living from their tropical garden, using only hand tools, and from selling fish caught during daily fishing excursions. They explained to me how they had learned to embrace basics, growing pineapple, collecting coconuts, mangos, and catching grouper and lobster. They also schooled me on methods of tropical gardening, which requires different techniques from northern hemisphere gardens. These two embraced each day to the fullest, enjoying busy work intrinsic to their lives, as this couple pursued self-sufficiency. Many similar people live in Belize, a poor county as things are presently gauged. There

AN ASCETIC LIFE

is a certain feel to this place; like time travel to an earlier era. Mango Creek is an isolated village with fishing as its main income source, and this village had no electricity, save a generator that powers the fish processing plant in order to freeze fish awaiting transport. They have a 4000-gallon cistern for collecting rainwater; there are no wells, as the village is too near salt water for conventional freshwater wells.

One late afternoon I watched a group of young boys and girls in an open field playing softball, it was such a joy to observe this; they were having a wonderful time, cheering each other, and laughing. There was no television at that time in Mango Creek, no movie theatres; entertainment was created using imagination and what was available. One interesting observation during my three months in Belize, I did not see a single obese person. Consumptive glut is nonexistent in Belize.

Ascetic living can open life's dimension blocked by the blinding lights of materialism forming distraction, causing drift toward excess, as materialistic mentality becomes God like and controlling. Where do we draw the line of separation? What exactly is luxury and comfort? How is financial security properly defined? Definitions and examples are manifested by social patterns and influences. I had a good business quarter one particular year, creating a yearning for a certain car that socially reflects success. I purchased the car and in a short time, the intensity of my yearning dissipated, the car came to mean nothing to me other than a manner of getting from point to point. My yearning formed by how I perceived society would judge me, how I would fit into the material imagery design and escalating perceived acceptance within the established social format.

HINTERLAND JOURNAL

Historically the world's most influential teachers, sages and spiritual leaders practiced asceticism. It was the root of their omnipotence, an important energizing force, driving ability to discover spiritual inner awareness, allowing opportunity to impel teaching by example. Jesus displayed anger when the moneychangers set up business inside the temple. Jesus and Buddha were epitomes of ascetics, and the great Persian poet Rumi followed an ascetic theme. Mildred Norman, known as Peace Pilgrim gave up material wealth entirely and walked the highways of North America for nearly 30 years covering in excess of 25,000 miles. Not as protest but as a teaching method of simplistic living as an avenue toward global peace. Mildred accepted no money on her sojourn, only food and shelter handing out notes of wisdom during her time. "It's those who have enough, but not too much who are the happiest." Others, like Thoreau, Mother Teresa, and Gandhi and in his later years Tolstoy, embraced ascetic living. Why is this? Because this is where love and spiritual growth are truly discovered. Ancient cultures harmonized because they lived abreast of nature and throughout nature asceticism is practiced. Nature embraces essentials, always seeking only basic needs. Asceticism is where one feels the most profound power and purpose of life.

Thoreau said: "Simplify, simplify." Sums it up in two words.

Our Relationship to the Future

A few months ago I was researching for an essay on the cycles of the sun learning about the billions of years it has taken to achieve its present size, and its continual expansion, eventually achieving a red giant phase and then diminishing in size becoming a white dwarf star. I mentioned this study to a correspondent and how earth will perish during the red giant phase as the sun encompasses the earth's orbital zone. His response: "Why is this important? None of us will be alive."

Of course his observation is partly correct, we will not be here, but the importance of the distant future and distant past has bearing on present day life. If it were not for evolutionary cycles we would not be alive. Therefore, what happened early on created now, created us. At this historic point we represent the present, and as a species project an influential force driving forward toward the future, and possibly a distant future. The cycles of the distant past plants a notional seed germinating into what has occurred thus far and what can be predicted to happen, thereby profoundly influencing Earth's inhabitants during the human period. Our lives are enhanced by an awareness of planetary movements and the magnitude of the past, present and future. Knowledge of Earth's timeline adds dimensional thoughts, creating spiritual consciousness as well as real time cognition of life on our planet, its meaning and purpose.

My dogs, Orion and Venus, and I have a few favorite trails

in the nearby state forest, and one-trail transits the bank of a creek, Burkhart Creek. This creek meanders, and one particular turn offers a nice resting point. The forest workers have placed a picnic table there, but it is seldom used, because this is a hike-in spot and the typical picnic folks are drive up oriented; so, this spot is sort of our personal place. There is sedimentary build up on the inside portion of the creek's turn, where we have discovered several geodes.

Geodes occur in abundance in only five states: Indiana, Iowa, Missouri, Kentucky and Utah. They are mostly baseball size or a bit larger, round stones with hollow interiors composed largely of quartz. Rock hounds collect them, saw them in half exposing the glitter of the internal quartz, and then polish the edges for use as paperweights or other ornamental functions. Geodes are products of geological activity during the Mississippian Age, and are approximately 340 million years old. As I hold one of these discoveries in my hand, the sensation of its long history magnifies the emotion of the moment. This geode was intact, as it is now, when the first humans appeared 2-3 million years ago, and it was 337-338 million years old at that time. It challenges the imagination to fathom such a span of time.

Living organisms offer us a more personal connection, relating to timelines, with less imaginary strain. The giant Sequoia is one example of grasping the reality of time as a comparison to present day. The General Sherman tree (a Sequoia) is between 2300 and 2700 years old. The Sequoias were slaughtered by human intervention during the 19th and early 20th centuries, and were threatened with extinction. The Sequoias are not the oldest trees, but are likely the most spectacular of the older species. There is one spectacularly beautiful evergreen Cyprus tree in Iran, the Zoroastrain Sarv that is 4500 years old about the same age as Stonehenge. The oldest known living tree is a bristle-cone pine named the Methuslah Tree (4700 years old) located in Inyo National Forest in California, it was alive when the first pyramid was built.

Why is all of this meaningful? I believe that knowledge of life and its cycles in relationship to time allows perspective, opening truths and knowledge that can be applied to our journey as a species. We have stumbled in so many ways as we make our walk with time, gaining balance and stability as our timeline gains momentum and understanding. Destruction must become more vivid regarding its power to languish and stagnate. If we are to be a presence similar to the geode we must adjust to the challenge of longevity, blend antiquity with destiny. It seems possible.

The Grace of Companionship

Companionship's define life. The first thought is long-term human partnerships. Sharing each day, attached, viewing the bond as a singular entity, interacting in dual servitude toward goals and purpose. Frequently such arrangements are out of balance, but when things are in sync it's the best of the best.

Companionship's extend beyond human pair bonding ubiquitously displayed throughout the Universe. Earth has its moon. Jupiter has four major moons and the giant star Sirius has a tiny companion star named by astronomers Sirius B, which travels a fifty-year orbit around its companion. Our solar system is a blip on the universal screen with its planets serving as companions held in place and fed by the Sun. Earth is 4.5 billion years old with life forms appearing around one billion years ago, formed by the Sun's expansion warming the Earth. Prior to Sun's growth Earth was a barren place. Our companionship with the Sun created us. Human's now number in billions; yet, connected in thoughts, spirit and life spans forming a massive organism and companionship. Anthropologists are astounded how ancient cultures separated geographically evolving with social similarities. Presently the global human community has yet to discover cohesive harmony, but if and when it does, boundless worth will enhance meaningful values, direction and purpose.

Nature forms the most profound companionships,

THE GRACE OF COMPANIONSHIP

reaping its many benefits. Envision the wolf without its pack and observing a pair of bluebirds in spring as they carry nesting material, each carrying a load is pure delight. Wildflowers and their pollinators are companions. A pair of Canada geese occupies warm months near my home, flying from pond to pond, always in voice and never more than a few feet apart. Beavers build communal housing displaying engineering skills and teamwork. No union contract negotiation required. Dens and nests are homes, a base element attached to earthbound companionships.

Humanity has experienced vivid changes over long, historical spans of time. Science unearths details studying early human sociology revealing harmonious cohabitation, embracing Earth's natural gifts, coalescing intuitively. During early human development populations were greatly dispersed forming small units, dependent on compatible day-to-day function and communal unity for survival sharing goals toward life's continuation.

As populations expanded dispersal became concentrated, massing to greater degrees in selected geographical areas. This activity escalated in Mesopotamian regions clinging to local river systems, becoming less nomadic than earlier hunter-gatherer tribes. This opened opportunity for great change in basic living designs, restructuring social patterns, which remain in place during this modern era. Agricultural sophistication advanced; animals were domesticated as a food source and hunter-gatherer cultures dissipated. From this fresh concept changes continued to develop. The establishment of geographic boundaries causing social separation and fears of border breach intensified. Sagacious tribal wisdom of sharing the Earth's gifts was overpowered. This new design emphasized government's controlling influence, outlining communal direction. Consumption fell under the control of government dispersal; monetary systems were installed, following legislated guidelines as food was now purchased. Individual survival and quality of life transpired based upon one's ability to acquire monetary and material wealth, fusing with controlled distribution procedures. This early, historical civil adjustment represents the beginning of humanity moving away from natural earthly attachment, seeking creation of its own environmental composition, fashioning isolation from the harshness and challenges of nature. The Bronze Age advanced agricultural implement development, melding with increasing war mentality as fears escalated regarding border encroachment. Farming tools were redesigned as weaponry; harvesting sickles became swords to equip massive armies. Horse drawn hauling carts evolved into chariots of war. A quest to dominate and control grew from this condition and has remained solidly in place since this time. However, chariots and swords have been replaced with more efficient devices.

So, how does companionship play into this? Our companionship with the Earth has been altered, viewing Earth's gifts as a means of enhancing human comforts. Exploitation has replaced congruity, pillaging resources, polluting air, water and soil displaying unquenchable drive to add dimension to collective comforts and materialistic impulse. Simplicity has been lost, leaving in its wake a consumerist's "grab bag", as the bottomless pit of craving extends far beyond basics, viewing the vista of life as one of accumulation, hoarding, in a display of superficial worth.

THE GRACE OF COMPANIONSHIP

Are there simply too many people? In my view, it seems possible that as a species developing so far technically solutions surely can be accomplished. It's a matter of understanding negative issues, forming changes based upon human applied intelligence moving to new plateaus of logic. Our errors are obvious. It seems possible to return to a harmonious companionship with Earth. It's apparent that if we are capable of installing an incredible rover on Mars, transmitting amazing, clear photos, we should be able to grow our food without drenching crops and soil with toxins that without the slightest doubt poison our food and our bodies.

Many seek bliss within material wealth. This is a misconception. Materialism has creped its way into influence from surface portrayals popularized by modern society. We are inundated by socially manifested, celebrity imagery flaunting outrageous behavior preying on undeveloped, youthful minds.

I have two loving, intelligent dog companions, they experience each day living in the present. They don't own anything, nor desire to own anything; yet, are fulfilled with a euphoria of being alive. I try to emulate my life in this fashion, seeking introspection, placing less value on the complexities of socially infused materialism. I can never develop to the place my dogs are, but reduction exposes a comfort zone. It's a pleasant place to experience life, a companionship with oneself.

Consumption

When I was a kid during the fifties, our town had many stores, mostly family owned and operated, and these stores were designed to fulfill particular consumer needs. Clothing stores, supermarkets, sporting goods, and also gas stations individually owned with vehicle service equal in importance to selling gas. Department stores were only found in larger cities and it was a special event to travel to Columbus and ride the escalators at the Lazarus department store. I lived in a smaller town, Marion, Ohio about forty miles north of Columbus. We dressed in our Sunday best for these excursions. The mid-west during that era was a fascinating place to experience youth.

In this modern era things have evolved into quite a different shopping climate. We no longer have stores, we have institutions with acre size buildings, which house every imaginable consumer item in organized rows with signage to direct customers, and phones located at strategic locations to call for assistance to locate a particular item. A fleet of electric, riding shopping carts is available for those unable or unwilling to combine a day hike with their shopping experience. And forget the dressing up idea to go shopping. It is now more of a dress down event.

Consumption is an interesting word. It covers a spectrum of pursuits even when we breathe we consume air, which is a necessity for life. We also will die without water and food.

CONSUMPTION

These are necessary consumptions.

Questions arise regarding consumption other than those necessary for life. Consumption conflict can cause imbalance as wants and needs intertwine creating an elusive line of distinction regarding needs and unnecessary wants. Many factors can play into this equation. We are surrounded by influences, directly and indirectly. The purveyors of consumer commodities design and calculate like mad scientists to influence consumers to purchase more and more creating markets that reach far beyond basic needs and function causing present day consumption to grow into a monstrous entity. The condition of present day consumption reminds me of the novel written by H. G. Wells (1895) The Time Machine. The plot is based on a scientist who invents a time machine and ultimately becoming a time traveler arriving in the year 800,701 AD discovering a beautiful but mindless race of people the Eloi. This race spent their days in leisure idleness, and his first experience with them was seeing a woman drowning in a nearby river, struggling for her life, as her fellow Eloi lounged on the riverbank and paid no attention to her plight. The traveler was in disbelief and saved the woman himself. As the story unfolds it was disclosed that the Eloi were under the control of another race, the Morlocks, which lived underground in caves, troll like beings. At intervals a siren would sound and the Eloi became entranced and would walk in a semi-conscious state toward to the sound of the siren and enter the Morlock cave to be eaten by the Morlocks. The Eloi were like cattle, harvested by the Morlocks.

I see similarity to this story unfolding in today's over consumptive culture, which is greatly influenced by the sirens of clever and manipulative marketing techniques. Consumer choices have grown exponentially in choice and availability adding dimension and confusion simultaneously. The human mind can be twisted and manipulated in various ways, we can become entranced similarly to the Eloi, falling victim to wants injected into our veins by astute, psychologically implanted marketing. The difference is the modern day Morlocks are feeding us instead of eating us. Foods are purposely enhanced through clever processing designed to trigger addictive cravings that have nothing to do with nutritional needs. The modern day, highly processed foods are directed at satisfying emotional cravings for certain foods and chemical additives. The Morlock marketers have gained knowledge how to increase food consumption, and it is working well. The obesity epidemic is an obvious result. The same technique is used in marketing the wonders of technology, the device you have in your hand was outdated at the time of purchase. The high tech folks have new, updated versions waiting in the wings, as they allow the old ideas time for market marinating, establishing a place, then they bring on the next generation device and the consumer is tempted (required?) to upgrade. It's the Morlock siren of manipulation using a market desire creation playing on peer pressures and the sheep mentality that has crept into present day culture. "Got to have one of those!"

So, what do we do? I suppose we must evolve in a similar fashion that we have historically. Become more individualistic, much like our ancestors and previous generations. Knowledge of exactly what is happening is a good place to start. Discover individual patterns of consumption countering Morlock marketers. Options do exist, good options if we take time and thought to seek them out. Food consumption is an excellent place to begin the change. Locally grown fresh, whole foods are still available. Think through decisions regarding gadgets and devices, evaluate needs over spontaneous response to every new twist and turn technology offers. High-end technology is ingrained in our culture, and it is here to stay. It's all about change, adaptation and logical approaches. It can be done.

Eco-logical

In the late 60s I lived in San Francisco and often would take the ferry to Sausalito and then take the shuttle bus to Muir Woods, a magnificent sanctuary of mature redwood trees. This is such a special place to visit. Walking the busy main path, just ahead of me, was a nice looking family, husband and wife with three young children. They were well-dressed and obviously upper middle class. The father stated looking at the majestic giants, "You see one redwood, and you've seen them all." To him this was a logical observation, and as one views many elements of nature it exposes uniform patterns, it's one of nature's functions, repetitive duplication. What is clearly obvious, is this man's observation rings a tone of indifference, lacking ability to understand the precise spectrum these trees represent, their history and overall importance to this particular natural composite melding in union with less dominate life forms, thriving and evolving because of the existence of this grove of giant trees. Often the human species reacts to nature and its importance with shadow thoughts, forming opinions without the light of knowledge displaying a broader more significant perspective.

Historically natural treasures have become victims of intense human exploitation, to a greater degree in what is referenced as "modern times." It's difficult to define the exact line representing the beginning of "modern times." Although, it is a safe assumption those living in the present would define this era as "modern times." I once saw an old photograph, taken in the late 19th century, with groups of men standing among hundreds of stumps of redwood trees, some were holding very long cross-cut saws, and large axes, and lying on the ground were giant redwood logs. To each of these men, and also the lumber baron that financed the operation, this was a logical event, a display of conquest, as they displayed pride in their accomplishment. In my view this was a holocaust, willful destruction of life that had flourished and survived for thousands of years.

The animal most closely resembling humanity are locust, swarming and devouring all life in its path addressing their immediate personal agenda, with no regard for preservation. The difference is locusts are intermittent invaders, and human invasion is continual. As the rail system began its movement west, passengers would randomly shoot wild buffalo from windows of the passing train, and the buffalo died by the thousands, their bodies rotting in the sun. This was considered great sport for these passengers, and seemed perfectly logical to kill these wild animals. This type of twisted logic carries on today, less vivid but no less destructive. We also now have resistant movements of intervention tagged as radical, more of a nuisance than a worthy alternative highlighting negative destructive practices. Economics is at the forefront of political and social environmental preservation efforts. When we had the horrific oil spill in the Gulf of Mexico, it clearly displayed the illogical decision to drill for oil in this area. The campaign to stop drilling was short lived, beaten down by lobby groups blackmailing the public with threats of 10 dollar a gallon gasoline if drilling ceased. Of course this is untrue, but to the lobby groups and the recipients of this message, it was logical.

In the late 40s and early 50s we randomly sprayed DDT without forethought, nearly causing the extinction of the Peregrine Falcon. When the loge pole pines were threatened by the loge pole beetle the knee jerk reaction was to spray poison on the beetles, which would kill endless numbers of birds that feed on these beetles. Famed naturalist, Adolph Murie wrote a lengthy paper on why the beetle should be allowed to function, explaining how this encroachment was a natural cycle for the trees. This intervention by Murie saved the beetles, birds and trees. Those that supported spraying thought it was the logical thing to do. At intervals there is talk of a hydro-electric dam to be constructed on the Yukon River, creating a low cost energy source to attract industrial growth to Alaska. This dam would destroy the Yukon Flats entirely, which is the nesting ground for $1/6^{th}$ of North American waterfowl. To economic speculators and dam builders, this would be logical.

Chemical use is now omnipresent in farming practices; each year farmers' saturate their fields with pesticides, herbicides, and chemical fertilizer. This practice has been in place for many years. The soil is saturated with these invasive, artificial substances that eventually filter into the food, and are being absorbed through human consumption. Bees are dying at a staggering rate ingesting chemicals as they attempt to pollinate. To the farmer, and producers of these chemicals this spraying is logical. Economically manifested and driven.

The potential for economic gain trumps logic. Long-term effects are ignored. Selfishness and a collective drive toward self-serving agendas represent the thrust of modern society.

ECO-LOGICAL

Listening to political candidates as they speak to their potential voters, you hear nothing about preservation of Earth functions, or conserving. What you hear is ongoing rhetoric directed at individual economic potential gains, the distribution of tax revenue, and how if they are elected positive change for the better is just on the horizon. As global population growth inundates our planet, we are moving quickly toward large scale, self-inflicted damage and potential ruin. There are in place quality environmental movements, with knowledgeable and practical plans for positive change, exposing the damaging effects forthcoming from ignoring environmental preservation and its benefits. As a species, it is imperative that we begin recognition of need to harmonize with the Earth, conserve and support environmental protective causes. Without the natural cycles and functions of nature, without clean, pure water, air and natural food sources, there are no positive elements to our future. It's logical. Eco-logical.

Endangered

Earthly organisms are on an odyssey of survival, a perpetual force, ranging from annual migrations to million year evolutionary cycles. Life form composition is elemental and uniform, imprinting, configuring, and unfolding in multiplicities.

When dinosaurs dominated Earth with an unyielding grasp on functions of survival and reproduction, it would have been unimaginable that these large, powerful, creatures could be considered endangered, at risk of extinction; yet, when a cosmic collision poisoned the atmosphere they died, disappearing from Earth's surface. Lesser species, especially subterranean dwellers fared better. Dinosaurs became extinct millions of years before humans appeared.

Over the span of human history reshaping has occurred, climate change, axis shifts, ice ages and infinite movements of earth's stratum. All species face risk of extinction, often recovering, but risk is a resolute, tenacious constant.

The human has replaced the dinosaur's dominance, displaying power exceeding all previous influential presence. Human intrusions are vast and destructive, invading the earth's crust as intervention ventures forth undaunted. This domination and control leaves a wake of devastating consequence on the environmental fabric of the planet. Humans killed thousands of passenger pigeons (extinct since 1914), and slaughtered buffalo shooting from windows of passing

ENDANGERED

trains as a form of entertainment leaving their corpses to rot in the sun. Clubbed baby seals to death for their fur to satisfy social vanity, pillaged forests, clear-cutting resulting in destructive soil erosion. The air and water have been polluted as the species drives forward for economic gain, posturing in gluttonous orientations. The soil is now laden with deadly chemicals designed to increase yields at less cost, producing greater profit for farmers poisoning land, crops and beings. This endeavor may prove irreversible. These processes of human intervention ring a tone of endangerment. Endangerment is the first step toward extinction.

Large cities display negatives influenced from excessive population densities. Social dysfunction is highlighted within congregated masses. The regression is obvious, as separation of class and wealth magnifies implemented through political and social indiscretion. The reaction is to look to governments for needs and solutions. Governments were conceived as forces to unify and organize toward betterment. Largely this has failed, as governments become corrupted and misdirected by influential outside forces with self-serving agendas. Economics trumps compassion and preservation.

As the modern world is shaping, human manifested destructive practices are ubiquitous and risk is escalating conversely. Human growth and expansion endanger many species of plants and animals; however, these practices are also an endangerment for the human species itself. The human is a warring being, developing weaponry capable of destroying, not only millions of people, it can destroy the atmosphere, plant and animal life, pollute water, soil and air. War is an ingrained concept. Vividly apparent observing the festering hate among global ethnic cultures displaying intolerance and anger, predicting war's inevitability and the use of mass destructive weaponry, which has been historically demonstrated.

As a species we recognize our lack of harmony, as the forces of our spiritual presence opens options and alternatives. Spiritual leaders speak of compassion and love; values delivered from an inner source, exposing dynamics capable of overcoming omnipresent human convoluted failures. Can these forces quell the chaos? It is a hope, and does seem possible, but until this flow dominates endangerment prevails.

Essentials

As societies expand wants and needs change, interests develop toward agendas designed by the character and social structure of a given era. Individual challenges and goals form, as cultural momentum flows with a transforming energy.

At this time in human history advanced technological devices are attached to our lives leading us to their dependency. Technological advancement has been apart of human development since the discovery of fire; this is not a new phenomenon; however, the magnitude of modern technology is on a greater scale; speed of task has grown exponentially and usage is in essence more diverse and dominate on all levels. Some view this onslaught of technological growth as invasive, worrisome, instilling fear and uncertainty. Change historically is seldom openly welcomed.

About 20 years ago I found this great dictionary at a yard sale, bought it for one dollar. I loved this dictionary; it became an essential fixture in my life, leafing through the pages seeking a better word of expression. That dictionary now is on the bottom shelf of my bookcase, covered with a layer of dust and has a forlorn look. Presently my writing is done on my computer, I click an icon in the applications file and it instantly opens a dictionary with a box to type in the word I am seeking. This is such an amazing tool. I click an adjacent box and access a thesaurus list for my chosen word; however, my old dictionary will remain on my bookshelf, it still has value. As wonderful as my computer is it needs power, which can be lost for various reasons, and my old, one-dollar dictionary will then come to the rescue. Many high tech devices are similar, they work well until they fail, and then we must revert to old stuff. It's my guess that old stuff will always be around; maybe the new stuff now in place will become old stuff. Things just seem to eventually drift that way.

The downside to this high-speed onslaught of clever devices is that they tend to overpower recognition of the ordinary, simplistic essentials, which are the root foundation of our inner selves. Essentials are also necessities, influences, guiding us to our desired destinations. Technology certainly can be a contributor and will continue to affect our lives in a myriad of ways far into the future; thereby it is essential that we learn to adjust to it in manners of understanding, where and how to use it without allowing it to impair our spiritual presence and growth. Human life forms require essential elements reaching far deeper and multi-directionally than handy devices can take us.

In order to reach a higher plane of thought and touch the presence of introspection, it is imperative that we view the Earth wholly, not confined in a cage of circuits and beeping sounds. Many are trapped in urban zones, live in squalor among polluting forces, a matrix of life confined and controlled by an environment of human creation. As one lives in such a manner a tolerance for this life increases, manifesting into acceptance. Cities are where commerce and enterprise have germinated, with hubs of transport and distribution, huddling to embrace fiscal growth, spawning overconsumption. Some may view this as essential in our modern world, as our society has drifted into materialism, creating complexities of questionable purpose and magnitude. It is a hope that cities can become less pollutant, discovering balance with earthly beauty and function, and there is movement toward this change. Social separation may ultimately not exist, a world without walled, gated communities and so much fear of one another.

The impetus of our modern world directs us toward physical idleness, collectively we sit, an activity that our bodies reject. The design of modern food choices creates additional negatives as essential nutrients are processed out of foods, and artificial, chemical enhancers are added to trick the body and mind into a false sensation of satisfaction, increasing cravings for these processed foods, adding to the obesity epidemic that has inundated modern culture. The body becomes confused as it is fed calories without essential nutrients; it reacts by storing these calories in the form of fat, and is being starved while it increases in size. The conundrum of consumption and the nutritional void are likely the most prolific negatives that exist in modern society. Whole foods, grown locally, ingested regularly, in proper portions offer solution, allowing taste cravings to move back to their natural state and health is restored. Balanced and proper nutrition is an absolute essential to our future, and it has little to do with technology.

Evolutionary processes are miraculous forces, as the tides of life rise and fall in a cadence of change and betterment. Expansion is inevitable; it's a dynamic unto itself, as we individually ride our waves of destiny. The essentials are essential.

Falling Back To Butterflies

Three summers past we experienced a horrid drought. Crops failed, ponds dried up and grass was brown, an apocalyptic scene. The poplar trees took the biggest hit; we lost ten yet some survived, a depressing summer. The forces of nature can be gentle or harsh; they can display extreme beauty or hideous ugliness. Regardless of crisis magnitude nature perpetuates, adjusting and regenerating, harmonizing with Earth, flowing with tides of change.

Observing those dying poplar trees I felt despair and anxiety; however, in nature death creates momentum. In nature, death channels life. Humanity also, if one lives a long, fulfilling life with love, joy and purpose their legacy reflects in offspring's moving life to a higher place.

Human life is connected to nature's functions but in recent times has fell out of natural rhythms, causing imbalance. Early humans were like the eagle and fox; they killed to feed their young, securing their future. They foraged for wild plants in nature's garden thriving from direct attachment to Earth's natural offerings. Progression over long spans of time caused humanity to distance itself from Earth's spiritual presence seeking to alter environments, adjusting to an expanding populous. These events slowly created a different approach, requiring living in closer proximity, forming conglomerates of population densities defined by geographic boundaries.

FALLING BACK TO BUTTERFLIES

This new design isolated itself from wild places. Governments formed, agriculture expanded, accommodating the new social structure becoming incapable of self-sufficiency. Monetary systems were installed as a distribution method of basic needs. Humanity became reliant on governments, conforming to urban entrapment. These changes shaped the root ideology of the modern era.

Consequence from these redirections raise questions. Anthropology reveals humanity has occupied our planet for approximately two million years and present day arrangement has been in place for around fourteen thousand years, beginning in the Fertile Crescent. This is also the birthplace of large-scale war, and the perceived need to amass armies for invasion, control and dominance and to defend against neighboring aggressors. Hunter-gatherer cultures leave no artifacts resembling this condition. Early tribal cultures were widely scattered, did not recognize borders, functioning in small units relying on earthly gifts, flourishing in cohesiveness. Massive armies and large-scale war had no place in early social structure.

War has become a firm fixture in modern culture, and continues to escalate. When Hitler was at his peak of greatness he viewed war's power as the ultimate mechanism of control and manipulation. He gained this power through political posturing, falsely convincing an entire country that his guidance will lead to utopia. How often has this scenario gained prominence? Hitler represented evil, and after his demise the collective feeling was peace was finally achieved. As I read the daily news this is an incorrect assumption. Upheaval and senseless killing continues. Children killed with poison gas delivered by the leader of their own country. Young girls kidnapped to be sold into slavery, abused and offered for ransom. How is this considered an improved design from what the ancients had in place for such a long period of time? Of course it is not. A question presented to me was: "Are we supposed to go back to primitive life picking daisies and spearing fish?" It would seem logical, but also impossible, although I question the term primitive, and I do doubt ancient cultures had time for daisies, the struggle for survival consumed them. We, as a species have reached the tipping point and solutions remain elusive.

Over the past ten years I have lived in a natural place far from metropolitan zones. My daily connection to nature has become imbedded in my soul. The quiet, peaceful day-to-day life has no resemblance to urban noise and clutter. I feel more in balance than during working years, mired in congestion, placing money at the forefront. Nature is perfection, and as one connects to nature more profoundly this vivid reality comes into focus; the morning rattle of the woodpecker, a flock of loquacious crows transiting the sky. This particular spring is most welcome after an exceptionally harsh winter. My favorite spring critter is the butterfly, flitting from place to place, probing with its delicate, single sensitive identifying finger. The butterfly is a product of nature's most fascinating metamorphosis and as my life progresses it has become apparent our species is in dire need of re-design, new direction and transformation away from the ubiquitous imbalances of present day society. With its vivid color and motion the butterfly epitomized life and the beauty of nature, wending forward, embracing its time on Earth. As I observe them dismay

FALLING BACK TO BUTTERFLIES

is tempered and I am spiritually lifted to a higher place, as nature is our quiet teacher and if we listen, learning its precision lessons we can mirror the butterfly, falling back to it, in a cadence of higher purpose and direction on a pathway toward more peaceful, spiritual bliss.

Fringe Benefits

When the subject of fringe benefits arises the first thought is an attachment to jobs excluding direct pay but worthy, indirect influences. These benefits are important considerations when evaluating employment opportunities. Some jobs offer no fringe benefits, with low wages, instability and questionable worth. Quality careers usually offer fringe benefits. Fringe benefits add stability and security day-to-day without laying hard cash in our hands.

Are not our lives kin to our jobs? Daily life unfolds in response to our environments, which is consistent among all earthly life forms. If we are born and raised in an inner city ghetto where crime and dysfunction are commonplace we follow this theme of living. Our surroundings dictate, influencing destiny. Fringe benefits can play important roles adding dimension and purpose to life. In a crime-ridden ghetto fringe benefits are indefinable. Early life fringe benefits are represented by guidance from parents and adult mentors.

Present day social structure is plagued with distractions. Observing the inundation of personal technological devices generates intrusion. How can one discover introspective depth and meaning if they are engulfed in electronic social media interaction? My grandson's girl friend is relentlessly communicating as she glances at her cell phone every minute, which is in her hand and permanently open to her Facebook page. It's

FRINGE BENEFITS

an obsession, forming a contraction, controlling, blocking out all else while consumed by frivolous, ongoing texting.

 The major flaw within modern times is urban entrapment canceling out thought processing outside of this zone. Cities deluged in noise, snarled roadways, life speeding forward toward expanding chaotic social trends. Values are formed based on monetary influence, creating class identity and separation, revering affluence and ignoring the downcast. Within this matrix thoughts of Earth's natural function are absent in the minds of the majority. "How much did that new I-phone cost?" "When will gasoline prices go down?" "When will politicians get their act together?" I'm wondering how many even know the sun exists, or contemplate our journey as an Earth bound species, where we came from and where we are headed. The fringe benefit of knowing and understanding our world in its completeness can open unending enlightenment adding immense value to the present and future, infusing recognition of life wholly. Nature, how we embrace it and understand it is of great importance to fulfillment toward gaining broader more meaningful goals. Knowledge and its applications are life's power brokers, an unshakable constant. Those high end I-phones and shiny new cars are cultural toys, which have little to do with inner discoveries located on the less vivid fringes of the glut-oriented plague.

 In mid October I traveled a 300-mile section of the Ohio River with my boat. It was physically and mentally challenging. As evening drew near I sought anchorage for the night. Most anchorages along this section of the river are in remote locations; many are adjacent to National Forests, or in the protection of an uninhabited island. Feelings of sanctity were present

HINTERLAND JOURNAL

as solitude opens the mind to higher consciousness. In such places one is detached from the tangle of human influence given opportunity to observe life functioning directly with Earth. One quiet evening along the shore of the small island where I anchored, three deer appeared and began to swim to the mainland, only a few hundred yards. This island was their sanctuary of safety. It was my guess this is a habitual, nightly swim to browse for food returning to their island near sunrise. I observed bald eagles, heron, coots and cormorants, all living and thriving among the natural gifts of the Earth. This experience offered divinity only found in such places.

Our civilization is likely to continue much as it is. Technology is ingrained. Has been since the discovery of fire. We cannot return to hunter-gatherer roots. We are challenged to assimilate, adjust, seeking enhancement to our daily embrace of life, blending and reaching out to nature in a fashion of appreciation and preservation allowing Earth's natural gifts to become as important as social goals. Nature offers a place of reverence above material accumulation, representing spiritual wealth, serving as an elixir to the stresses of modern culture. Fringe benefits.

Intentional Geometry

Today I have been thinking about geometric patterns and shapes, their intention and purpose, the obvious, the less obvious, and those, which are more ambiguous. I'm thinking about geometry's vast and profusely influential melding with Earth's functions and living forms, as patterns and shapes release intentional, visual pulsations activating a myriad of energizing forces which directly effect all earthly life forms.

Geometric designs are visible throughout nature. Some display distinct, symmetrical perfection, others are called fractals which are formed by fragmentation, splitting into parts, creating reduced-size copies of their original form, a process call self-similarity which can vary in degrees of duplication, often more abstract in shape and size, some forming less accurate duplications while others are more exact. Examples of fractals in nature include clouds, river networks, fault lines, mountain ranges, snowflakes, lightening, cauliflower, broccoli, systems of blood vessels, and ocean waves. Even coastlines may be loosely considered fractals in nature. Trees and ferns and also are clear examples of fractals. Artists are inspired by fractals; the renowned abstract artist Jackson Pollack often displayed fractals in his works.

I see spider webs daily in summer. A tiny creature on its mission of survival creates these devices. A single spider will often construct five webs each day, and then eats its web after serving its purpose in order to ingest protein, creating material for its next set of webs. These webs are images of beauty, especially when the morning sun strikes them glistening with dew, revealing geometric design perfection.

Honeybees are master craftsmen; their cells are prefect hexagons, constructed of micro-tolerances with each cell positioned at a 13-degree list to prevent the honey from tipping out prior to sealing it with wax. These tiny hexagons cells may vary in size. Cell dimensions are engineered to exactly accommodate the number of cells allowable within the comb's available construction site. Cell size variation is more common in wild hives because in manufactured hives the allotted construction space is uniform. Honeybees reflect evolutionary intelligence, which functions throughout nature.

Geometry is vividly displayed throughout the earth in special application, often in a direct relationship with human interaction. Some geometric forms and structures are linked to metaphysical speculation, suggesting mystery, lacking clarity regarding specifics of origin and presence. The Great Pyramids are examples, the how and why of there construction is a source of endless debate regarding intended purpose. It's a fascination that the Egyptians constructed these large, complex geometric structures displaying distinct, knowledgeable application of geometry.

The Romans struggled with geometry, (which was problematic because of the difficulties associated with the application of Roman numerals to solve complex calculations) and were probably incapable of constructing such large, precise pyramid structures. As a result of the Roman's inability to assimilate the principles of geometry the science stagnated for

INTENTIONAL GEOMETRY

2000 years, from the era of the Egyptian pyramid construction.

Finally, the Greek mathematician Euclid (325-265 BCE) conquered a clear understanding of Geometry. Conjecture is that Euclid was an intense student of Egyptian history and also lived much of his adult life in Alexandria, Egypt, speculating that his ability to absorb and understand the principles of geometry was connected to his Egyptian interests. Greece and Egypt had a long period of trade and cultural connections, which may also have contributed.

The base measurements on the Giza pyramid, the largest one, are within six-inches tolerances point to point; modern buildings of lesser dimension cannot hold such tolerances. The exactness of this large, complex structure continues to perplex modern architects. It does cause wonder.

The intricate design of many of nature's critters is another source of mystery and fascination. The common box turtle displays unique and beautiful geometric markings, extending onto its shell's lower flange. I always pause when I discover one of these turtles to examine these patterns, such perfection. The chambered nautilus also characterizes living geometry with its expanding spiral of distinct markings all along the shell's exterior, growing larger as the inhabitant of this shell moves to the next chamber, a true wonder of the deep. And if the shell is cut in half, it's revealed that the chambers are equally spaced in a perfect equiangular spiral.

Flowers and plants are directly connected to soil, water and sunlight, displaying distinct and uniform geometric patterns, flourishing with color that attracts pollinators', a great bonding of sun, earth and organisms in rhythmical, omnipresent symmetry.

HINTERLAND JOURNAL

Geometric wonders are captivating, unfolding with infinite varieties of shape and scale. Geometry and nature are meshed, moving forward in unison, emulating the geometric Universe. The abundance of these observations offer continuing proof that all life forms on our planet, and likely others, are wholly fused, ever evolving in a vast variety of patterns and shapes, intentionally geometric.

"The goal in life is to make your heartbeat match the beat of the Universe. To match your nature with nature." Joseph Campbell

Raymond Greiner

Goats In The Garden

Seeds were planted long ago, the soil was hard, and took great effort to spade and till, but the of seeds of change were planted. Great men and women toiled to nurture the benevolent beds of love and hope.

As the seeds germinated, sprouts of change inspired the gardeners; leaf and blossom offered new direction, with a distinct and open road for life's fulfillments, with purpose, and this newness felt so right. This garden produced abundance, releasing its powers in an array of choices; prosperity was harvested and the gardeners were rewarded with crops of principle, logic, and ethics. Character and values were root crops, producing faith as love ripened, opening hearts, allowing a vivid feeling of a spiritual presence, without clouds of doubt.

Then came the goats.

Pond Food

Walking the aisles of Rural King, the local farm and feed store I read the various labels on the multiple feed bags; sweet stuff for horses, scratch grain for chickens, meat bird, layer crumbles, chick Starter and at the very end of the aisle, a vividly white bag, off by itself on a small pallet labeled pond food. It's really fish food, but the label struck a chord in me.

Farm ponds are sanctuaries of life. Often small, providing water for livestock and a method of water storage for seasonal dry spells. Water can be pumped into tanks or used for watering gardens. Rural land designed for self-sufficiency centers on its water source.

My pond has become more to me than a farm function; it serves those purposes well, but also creates a source of introspection, a window, comfort zone and observatory of life. If you desire a special view of nature sit on the bank of a farm pond for a while patiently allowing your eyes to wander the water's surface revealing peaceful, subtle activity. Small swirls appear; may be a bluegill or turtle surfacing. The wind driven aerator forms a circle of bubbles, the ducks move about dabbling for various morsels, the water snake moves across the pond's surface with grace and speed, exits the opposite bank moving quickly seeking shelter in the tall grass. Frogs are abundant patiently awaiting their prey. As

POND FOOD

spring wanes cattails are forming with tails reaching for the sky. Dragonflies flit about, mesmerizing me as they fly in pairs, turning in unison with absolute precision. How can they do that?

One late winter, the pond thawed. Approaching the pond, I observed a small wake moving across the surface; upon exit from the water I could clearly see it was a mink, the first I had seen here, such a beautiful creature. It glanced my way, and then disappeared into the woods.

One summer day a caterpillar ventured onto a stick that was partially in the water. As the caterpillar inched onto the stick it floated away from the bank, becoming marooned. The caterpillar then walked toward the end of the stick and it began to tip into the water from its weight, it then walked to the other end of the stick and tipping repeated. Finally the caterpillar moves to the center of the stick, achieving balance remaining in place. Eventually the stick floats back to the pond's bank and the furry critter re-gained access to its land comfort. It seems a lesson applying to human complexities. If one direction fails, try another, if that one fails also, go to center and wait.

This micro ecosystem has been an important part of my daily life, offering visual and spiritual pleasures. I have an old steel chair that sits under the oak tree next to the pond, weather beaten, sits out all winter. This chair predates the fancy canvas fold up chairs or the aluminum webbed seat ones, it has become an attachment to my daily life, (also represents a low priority project that has been haunting me to sand and paint this relic). As I rest there in the early PM with my dog companions, Orion and Venus, I feel blessed to have this connection with mind/earth, a rarity in today's high-speed culture. Pondering that pond food bag at Rural King, I feel a temptation to buy a bag, toss in the crumbles, stirring things up a bit. However, at this time, I am not feeding the pond, the pond is feeding me.

The Conundrum of Poverty

Poverty is an emotionally powerful subject. With few exceptions global human quality of life is structured from a base of economic opportunities hailed as modern civilization marching to a cadence seeking prosperity through enterprise, commerce and trade. Contemporary social design is a byproduct of early Mesopotamia referred to as "the cradle of civilization." Social patterns evolved from this base developing geographically mixed cultures in a mutual quest for fiscal gain. Economics, trade and enterprise are world encompassing with striking disparity and exclusion.

Poverty is described in three distinct categories:

"Absolute poverty" is the most desolate, without adequate food or shelter, barely surviving and often plagued with extreme hunger and death by starvation. Education and medical services are compromised or non-existent.

"Relative poverty" is a condition gauged according to a threshold established by income demography. US poverty is categorized as relative poverty. Relative poverty is less apparent, homelessness being the most visual circumstance. In Los Angeles County on given nights in excess of 80,000 people are homeless.

"Asceticism" is voluntary poverty used as a method of seeking spiritual consciousness and a plane of life in opposition to the omnipresent ambition for affluence through economic status, material gain and accumulation. Practitioners of asceticism vow poverty as a means of teaching, revealing meaningful values beyond infusion of wealth and abundance as sources of enlightenment.

Kenya and sub Saharan Africa display vivid, widespread examples of extreme, absolute poverty. Sordid conditions exist in many third world countries; however, statistically the degree is most pronounced in sub Saharan Africa. The film documentary: <u>The End of Poverty? Think Again</u> is a compelling revelation exposing the level of horror these places have become. Children gleaning trash heaps for anything of the slightest value. The little work available is slave labor type jobs with finite wages, taxed heavily by corrupt governments preying on the world's poorest of the poor. Many third world regions have abundant natural resources and industrialized countries have exploited these resources in order to produce manufactured consumer goods for global distribution and economic gain. Large loans were pressed upon these impoverished countries under the guise of development projection, which has never manifested as industrialized countries continued to extract resources without implementation of self-sustaining commerce leaving a residue of extreme debt without ability to reduce the debt. Corrupt governments claim the need for high taxation in order to pay the debt, which is not occurring thereby suffering, continues.

Countries achieving economic success and prosperity have melded manufacturing and consumption. This formula relies on an expanding rate of consumption. If consumption dwindles, economies dwindle. In present day America excessive consumption is ubiquitous. There is an urgent drive to expand

THE CONUNDRUM OF POVERTY

manufacturing and consumption as a means of strengthening economic conditions. Questions appear regarding this social design. Is this balance or imbalance? The collective mentality is, "I have earned everything I own." A more honest assessment would be, "I have been given opportunity to succeed." Opportunity does not exist in sub Sahara.

So, where are the answers? Will disparity continue and increase? Charitable food donations given to oppressed countries are pilfered and sold by corrupt, ruling powers. Some would say this is a natural process as the Africans are incapable of competing. Africa was much slower to be influenced by the new civil design remaining a cohesive hunter-gatherer culture far longer than Europeans. When I see old photos of tribal Africa I see an extremely self-reliant race of people, harmonious and thriving for thousands of years in a harsh and challenging place. These are very strong people, likely the strongest in the history of humanity. The tribal villages and housing of ancient Africa were far more inviting and comfortable than the hovels of tin and cardboard that modern civilization has bestowed upon them. No culture has been more exploited than the Africans. The English came first, seized their land, killed their game for sport, and brought an entirely new living design, forcing radical change upon them. Enslaved them, sold them, continuing exploitation today as natural resources are pillaged without reward, and the global glut feeds itself on commandeered wealth leaving a wake of unfathomable despair.

Natural forces are the source of all earthly endeavors; capable of overpowering human created dysfunctions. Healing will likely be presented naturally, uninfluenced by the Dow Jones Average or the Gross National Product. Humanity has moved away from its organic roots seeking idolatry ritual within material wealth. Early tribal cultures embraced communal uniformity, housing was equal, and the act of sharing was important to security and longevity. Hunter-gatherers were directly connected to the earth; life was sustained by earth's gifts creating harmony, which has been lost in the current living design. Globally we have fallen into ethical contraction, expanding intolerance and the ever-presence of war, questioning direction and purpose. If we as a species are unable to alter inequities, solutions will self-generate. It would behoove the onslaught, self-feeding frenzy of acquisition to seek greater balance and sensitivity gearing energy toward apportionment and equality. As a species we have proven an ability to invent and install highly complex, technical devices it would seem equally possible to install basic comforts to those in dire need. Compassion is not complex.

Winter Solstice 2010

Another milestone is upon us and it is cold, as I knew it would be. My largest complaint about the cold is the time consumed layering clothing and putting on insulated boots, they are much harder to get on and off than my hiking boots. It's a workout before I walkout. I stagger around my cabin in the early AM, joints and muscles are stiff, seems I might need a wheel chair more than my trekking poles, but since the trail is not handicap certified I must go with the poles, and do the best I can. The dogs look at me differently in the early morning, trying to figure out what's wrong with me, after about 30 minutes of grunting and staggering around I begin to appear more like a stable, functioning organism again, joints begin to loosen and the body gets back on track, moving with some semblance of grace and direction.

Once the dogs hit the door, they lose interest in the distraction of their pack leader's odd movements as they bolt into the cold, wintery, morning air. What it must be like to move with such speed and balance, even in the dim light of early dawn. They both live to run, only stopping to smell or pee and then off again. Life is pretty simple for those two. I follow their pattern of living more than they follow mine.

OK, here we all are once again, the world continues to turn in perfect transit, and this day we pivot from fall to winter. The metropolis of spring and summer critters are nowhere in sight, no newts in the shallow mud, only frozen ground. The contrast is vivid. I read that there are two hundred and twenty-eight separate and distinct muscles in the head of an ordinary caterpillar, allowing them the hard turning angles of their heads needed to dissect a leaf. As I thought of this I could not help thinking how unimportant this fact would seem if it arose in conversation at a social gathering in today's technically sophisticated society; yet, is equal in intricacy to the most complex human created device. Such discoveries are ubiquitous in nature.

2011 is near to popping into our lives, it's astonishing to contemplate. To think my memories can go back as far as 1945, what a long path it has been. So much has changed. Our telephone was considered a true luxury, no dialing device, you simply picked up the phone and told the operator what number you wanted, and often it was necessary to yell into the phone to be heard. We listened to the radio at night, until we got our first TV in 1952. Now we are inundated with devices of every imaginable description, some add positive dimensions. Some do not. One Internet news video showed an electronic pickpocket device that can read the credit card numbers in your wallet by just holding it near your pocket. Are we ready for this?

Last year the solstice was a bright moonlit morning, with snow glistening on the tree limbs. No snow this year, but traces remain on the ground from the last snowfall. Winter has set in; it will display its beauty and its wrath. Winter is not a gentle season as we struggle to keep our body temperatures in comfort zones.

What lies ahead? All kinds of doomsday stuff out there,

planet X is on its way to collide with Earth, and according to many, 2012 will be our last year as a species. This kind of stuff has been around forever. Science tells us that the Earth will burn up in a few billion years, as the Sun goes into its red giant phase, but it's likely the human species will be Universally distributed before that time arrives. Big meteor polluted the atmosphere millions of years ago, killed all large mammal life, including the dinosaurs, but smaller species survived. This all happened millions of years before humans appeared. To think that the Universe will allow Earth to peacefully revolve around a perfect sun indefinitely is simply not in the cards. I'm personally asking for another 10 years, Santa wrote me back and said "I can do that, with your help." I am willing.

Life is a path, there are long uphill treks, and long downhill treks, some flat, some rocky, but all beautiful if we take the time to look. People often get lost, are unable to locate an inner direction live within a void of personal spiritual presences falling into a flow of events disallowing appreciation of the deeper meaning and beauty of life. Worries and insecurities dominate; cultural pressures mount, exposing false, socially created needs to participate in the vogue of various designs. The power of money is controlling, driving us ever forward to obtain a plethora of material possessions. The glut runs wide and deep, blocking one's ability to reach beyond the shallowness of such mentality. True joy is profoundly greater within our spiritual presence, as we embrace the simplistic treasures of life. Look to family, look to nature, think like a child.

I never tire or watching the dogs do their big circle run around, most often Venus is the pursuer, taking an oblique path to intersect Orion, who is just a tad faster. They will wrestle and bite each other's legs, growling and snapping playfully. Then suddenly stop, and just stare at each other. Then shortly, the chase resumes, until I call them. I should say, these dogs have a good life. Be blessed.

HAPPY SOLSTICE g/m/w

Rapa Nui

Rapa Nui is the Polynesian name for a remote south pacific island approximately twenty five hundred miles South East of the Marquesas Islands. This island's first European discovery was by a Dutch exploratory expedition in 1722 lead by navigator Jacob Roggenveen. The Dutch expedition arrived on Easter Sunday attaching the name Easter Island. Rapa Nui is a small, remote island creating challenge to early inhabitants, not only to locate and inhabit the island but also to establish a developing culture. Rapa Nui's history goes much deeper than from the time of its European discovery. A mysterious and fascinating culture, thriving from around 1200 CE, a society manifesting from mass pilgrimages of Polynesian voyagers in a migration and population dispersal effort occurring during this early historic period. After settlement established, tribal leaders and priests became obsessed with the Polynesian ritual of carving large stone statues called Moai with abstractly haunting faces then moving these massive carvings throughout the island. There is much speculation and conjecture concerning the purpose of these omnipresent stone monuments. Some are forty feet in height weighing over seventy tons. Archeological science and discovery reveals no time in ancient history when such large stones were moved such distances with so few people; Moai are located up to seven miles from their quarry site. Oral legend describes priests with mystical powers allowing the stones to walk short distances each day arriving at their place of permanence. Ancient roadbeds are visible indicating pathways with no archeological evidence of wheels or pulley systems. Details of this mystery remain in a void of speculation. These Moai carvings and placements would have been a remarkable feat even if only a few were present, but Rapa Nui has nearly 900 of these monoliths, all facing inland, away from the sea in a stark gaze as if searching in vain for their creators.

Early Rapa Nui inhabitants were from Polynesia, likely the Marquesas Islands. Voyagers from a distant island chosen in childhood engaging in lengthy preparation for their impending voyage. Maps or charts were unavailable; knowledge regarding destination and voyaging methods came via oral descriptions from tribal elders, knowledge passed down from previous generations. The chosen potential voyagers were taught frugality, food and water rationing in preparation to endure extreme hardships during their impending voyage. The voyagers constructed large double-hulled sailing craft, applying years of labor using natural materials. The Polynesian philosophy of the sea differed from Europeans. Polynesians did not fear the sea; embracing its abundance becoming a cultural attachment. The voyagers were taught to read wave patterns, wind direction, constellations, the rising moon and setting sun served as navigational guides directing them to hypothesized destinations spoken of by in the elder's oral sailing directions. These great voyages occurred hundreds of years before Columbus. The objective was to establish self-supporting tribal life in Polynesian tradition, but first they must face an ultimate challenge to make a long and arduous passage. As estimated nearness to destination approached the voyagers watched the sky

RAPA NUI

for birds and the sea's surface for floating palm fronds, indicating imminence of land. Their passage was from west to east, against the prevailing winds, adding difficulty to the voyage. It is likely voyagers waited until a year of an El Nino shifting wind direction favorably for this passage. Comparing the manner of life today, it is unimaginable to vicariously share the emotions these voyagers felt. Their resilience, determination and courage are monumental.

When the voyagers finally nosed their craft on the beach of Rapa-Nui, the island was covered, every square foot with dense forest. The trees were the largest of the palm species, height exceeding 100 feet, millions of giant palms. These trees took a century to reach maturity.

Today Easter Island is a barren place, not a single tree is standing. Observing this condition challenges comprehension, pondering the historical contrast and its causes. Opinions vary regarding this deforestation. It was likely a combination of factors. The island's population grew, land was cleared for crops, and wood was used for housing, fire and canoes. Some conjecture a large amount of timber was consumed to move the giant Moai. The voyagers carried rats, which were used as a food source, common on voyages and also within the Polynesian culture. Rats multiply at a staggering rate when food is abundant, and the rats thrived on Rapa-Nui's tree's seeds, and roots. As deforestation escalated changes occurred creating loss of tribal harmony. Invasions from Chilean tribes reduced population causing descending unity. Springs dried up, wood became scarce. The culture was falling down, culminating with the absence of trees. The culture teetered on the brink of extinction. European exploitation came in the mid and late nineteenth century, many ancestors of the voyagers were imprisoned, some eventually returning to the island, but the quality of life was abysmal without defined tribal structure. Rapa Nui was not blessed with abundant, natural rivers found on many Polynesian islands, a young island, less than one million years old, formed from volcanic eruption, dependent on rainfall and small springs for water sources. Multiple factors contributed to present day conditions. Observing Rapa-Nui in its present state evokes sadness. However, detailed reasons for Rapa-Nui's demise are fascinating and important. The starkest reality highlighting failure of Rapa-Nui is the fact that it was solely from human intervention. How much of this loss resulted from poor conservation practices? How much can be blamed on natural consumption relating to population growth? Obsession with Moai carving and moving may have distracted from the importance of the land itself. Modern archeological data reveals that much of the devastation was caused by the rat infestation and inability to eradicate them, more accepted now than earlier studies.

Popular author Paul Bahn and co writer paleontologist John Flenley address the state of the island in their book <u>Easter Island, Earth Island,</u> conjecturing: "the person that felled the last tree could see that it was the last tree. But still felled it. This is what is so worrying. Humankind's covetousness is boundless. Its selfishness appears to be genetically inborn. Selfishness leads to survival. Altruism leads to death. The selfish gene wins. But in a limited ecosystem, selfishness leads to increasing imbalance, population crash, and ultimately extinction."

Islands like Rapa-Nui model micro planets, revealing loss or gain directly related to eco-management. In the case of

RAPA NUI

Easter Island it was a thriving, place of reverence and spiritual benevolence, exposing accomplishments of cultural magnitude presented in the mystical gaze of the Moai. The optic of time reveals that the dynamic of change moves gratuitously, an unshakable constant. Fragility is often unrecognized and ignored. The mysteries of Rapa Nui remain intact; however, its history reveals lessons that can be applied to humankind's future.

These historic occurrences stir fearful predictions regarding practices within present day social structuring, an ever escalating force, wending on a path of destructiveness, applying minimal consideration of consequence intensity. Our species development may experience eventual reversal as we venture slowly toward felling our last tree.

The Nature of Relationships

The broad definition of a relationship is when two or more concepts, objects or people are connected, forming a link or alliance; however, the concept of relationships and their applications can be infinite in scope, reaching wider and deeper than typically conceived. Modeled socially, relationships are identified as partnering of two people, cohabitating, or seeking the historic ritual of matrimony. Beyond popular definitions, relationships develop in variable designs, identities and dynamics.

Perceptively, it can be observed that the first relationship encounter is the search for a sense of inner discovery, relating to oneself. Since we are complex organisms, a tapestry of neuronal and physical structures, the challenge is to sort out and arrange this intricate body of cells, forming a foundation of personal stability. Obvious examples are the difficulties we experience as we transit life's stages, especially puberty. At early stages of life we lack a significant bank of experiences, clouding the self-discovery equation, reverting to instinct, which is often reactionary and convoluted. Questions and choices emerge during this time. What kind of person will our personal evolutionary process reveal? Early in life root personality traits are formed, molding character identity. Will we develop a desire to control others or become prone to being controlled? Will we learn a natural

THE NATURE OF RELATIONSHIPS

compassion? Will we extract joy from seeing others suffer or from helping others? Will we become givers or takers? It is a diverse package to sift out. Observing our present culture's overall relationship with itself, characterizations run the gambit, revealing a variety of results, multiple, collective traits, developed individually.

The Earth itself reflects relationships, and as with all relationships, bending, shaping and flexing are essential, generating perpetual adjustment and directional changes. Science calls it evolution. The Earth's evolutionary process epitomizes relationship perfection, demonstrating cycles occurring over billions of years, in concert with nature's presence and functions. Flowering plants have a relationship with their pollinators, sunlight, soil and rain. Within this amalgamation emerge results; forming a composite force of reproduction, exhibiting harmony, beauty and balance. Predators serve as check valves, controlling excessive population growth. All life forms on Earth intertwine, contributing to an ability to relate, forming and functioning within the design of a biological relationship created by Earth's rhythmic cycles.

As I personally transit my later phase of life, challenges remain vivid, important and ever changing. As during puberty, aging reveals barriers, questions and a renewed need for direction and inner development. Life's challenges now ring in a different tone, and even as aging creates certain wisdom, with a bank of knowledge unavailable to a younger person, there remains confusion and questions. Spontaneous reaction can again cause reverting to instinctual actions, and often convoluted. The path still wanders, and clarity can be elusive, as influences and conditions appear that were not present in youth. Events, circumstances and the environment of an aging person are far different than when one was working with the energy and dynamics of a young body and mind. The need for discovery of a relationship with oneself has re-emerged, and consequence still sought among questions. How do I adjust to my aging body? How do I adjust to the way I am perceived within the structure of a youth driven culture? How can I re-discover new drive to embrace goal oriented personal agendas? Where can I find inner bliss and fulfillment that appeared with such little effort during prime years? Relationship foundation remains an important element in life at all stages, but the aging stage magnifies the importance and also reveals the persistence of difficulty finding purposeful direction. The good news is: It can be done. The condition of a partner is a welcome, large and positive support column, but in my circumstance nonexistent. I have two dog companions that easily challenge any human companion in overall quality of value. These two, Orion and Venus live and function of a level above the human plane, they are in balance with themselves, at all times, in all circumstances. My relationship with these two canine critters is a bond that few people ever achieve on a human-to-human level. They live in the moment, they show joy and appreciation in all phases of their lives, they don't complain, ever, they don't worry about trivial things and are not influenced by the power of money, they are examples of perfectly balanced life forms. They are exemplary in character and function, ask for nothing, give their hearts and souls to please. They display the core of relationship power and purpose. They simply amaze me.

THE NATURE OF RELATIONSHIPS

The value of a relationship challenges clear description, it is a felt thing, a harmony within the hearts of those engaged, moving forward, hand in hand, with a desire to taste life in its many flavors. We all need relationships, betterment is found within quality relationships, a support, directing and guiding us to the fruitions we seek.

From the hinterland

The Last Dogwatch

The last dogwatch is from 18:00 to 20:00 the name attached because at the end of this watch the star Sirius, the brightest star, becomes visible. As darkness descends the helmsman's senses are magnified and during calm times the vessel's rhythm slows opening loneliness revealing the power of quiet solitude as the helmsman's mind wanders in contemplation.

Nature is varied and magnificent, with stark contrast in life forms of land and sea; however, similarities exist as we study the perfection of the sea's structure and magnitude of life. In my younger years I was blessed to read Rachel Carson's masterful work <u>The Sea Around Us</u> filled with visions of Earth's early years and the revelation of how evolutionary processes created Earth of today. This book, and others, opened my thoughts to the expansiveness of life that abounds in so many forms. These readings triggered a passion to become intimate with the Earth's spectrum of life.

So many features of our lives are directed and structured by social design, as if outlines were passed out in Jr. High School with specific directions leading us to a utopian life. There is much emphasis now on comfort, and staying within the boundaries of social agendas. Present day vogue-enhanced living shuns simplistic values. Our new technological world has in a sense imprisoned us, blocking our view, as devices move to direct us with their dominance.

THE LAST DOGWATCH

In the early 80s my wife Nancy and I built a 33 foot sailboat on the bank of the Ohio River, launched there and transited the Ohio and Mississippi Rivers, and with our three young children, sailed to Central America and stayed for three months in the small country of Belize. We were a family of voyagers. It was a memorable and magnificent experience, far removed from the general present day structure of things. Belize is such a pristine place, with a large reef that is teeming with sea life of every description. It seems so long ago. Now Nancy is gone, a victim of the evil cell, the kids are showing gray in their hair as I have now entered my 8th decade, but the memories of those grand days linger, a cherished time when we lovingly embraced the sea.

As we crossed the Gulf of Mexico I came on watch and the end of the last dogwatch, dozing at the helm, as the breeze was slight and the sea dark. The boat's movement was slow, barely enough wind to hold the sails taut, with only the faint noise of the bow slicing the calm water. Suddenly, "Whoosh" I nearly jumped out of my skin. A dolphin surfaced next to the boat, blowing out its hole, and then several more appeared, surrounding the boat, swimming next to us for about a half hour. Dolphins epitomize grace and beauty, as they rise directing movements with such speed and precision. These visitations are a common occurrence for sea travelers. Later the next day many more dolphins visited us, swimming near the boat allowing the kids to reach down and touch their heads. It was a perfect day, sunny and warm with a good breeze, we were moving at a good clip, no challenge to the dolphins, a clear sky and a deep blue color to the water, sharing this moment with these magnificent creatures as we traveled together was an indescribable, surrealistic moment. How many are given such an opportunity?

As we arrived at Belize and nosed our craft on the lee anchorage of an uninhabited key with many palm trees our emotions heightened. The clarity of the water allowed us to see our anchor, as if we were suspended in the air. It was a very special time of our lives. During the time of our voyage it was before GPS, using a sextant, taking daily noon sights and advancing the line of position at about 3PM, to get our estimated position. So different now, everyone knows exactly where he or she is. It's an astonishing development, but maybe the lack of knowing one's exact position adds a degree of dimension to the adventure.

So, here I am, at a rather lonely time of life, but not without goals and plans. I have a new dogwatch, but now with two real dogs. Orion and Venus are my best friends, we are guardians of each other, and we have plans. There is still a bit of wine left in the bottle, and I am keeping the cork in place until the time is right, and that time is nearing. The old timers who traveled the far north in winter with dog teams would gauge the severity of the nighttime cold by how many dogs they allowed inside their tent at night. It was either a two, three or four dog night. All of my nights now are two dog nights, regardless of the severity of the weather, and it is pure joy to share my life with these two. Orion is so smart and Venus can challenge him on that, but she has an advantage, he is totally smitten by her, gives her whatever she wants, even lets her play with his beloved Frisbee, he won't try to take it back, so fun to watch these two. The joys of life keep coming and coming and I am forever grateful.

Questions do arise, on occasion: Where exactly is the core essence of life? Is it wealth? Is it fame? Is it social status? It's a challenge to answer such questions. It seems to be a profusion of things. The emotional joys of seeing children grow and mature, planting a garden in spring, an interaction with a puppy or kitten, seeing a rainbow or wildflowers blossom, having a laugh with a good friend, a good meal, a glass of wine, a conversation that goes on and on with one that you love. It seems the good life is a conglomerate, a joining of the mind/body/spirit and often clouded or blocked by social clutter, noise and urban congestion. Maybe we become too busy, at times. The best of our beings comes from a deep place, within our spirit, an unexplainable force, but we know when it is present, revealing its pulsation, we feel it.

The Necessity To Transform

Progression is a deliberate dynamic, creating opportunity and discovery, a momentum unto itself. Renaissance enters with or without a welcome mat illuminating passage to transformation. The dynamics of change is a perpetuating, unyielding force exposing infinite new paths. Earth began as a fiery ball of gas, evolving into a planet teeming with life. One can observe transformations in all forms of life; also there is a progression of transformations within Earth's stratum, resulting in formations of astonishing magnitude. By the nature of its own inertia transformation remains an unshakeable constant.

I camped on the banks of the New River in West Virginia, in the presence of its majestic gorge. The entire gorge is solid rock, mostly granite. I emptied my canteen, spilling the water over a rock; it splashed and dissipated quickly running off the rock. As we wash our face with water, or drink it, we define it as a gentle substance, a soft liquid, with seemingly little power. Yet, when I view the New River Gorge, the realization is that this entire gorge was carved by only flowing water. 300 million years of time, the New River is second only to the Nile in age. I immersed myself in this glorious, breathtaking view revealing how time and water in unison created this massive transformation. Rock in the short-term is more powerful than water; however, teamed with time water can conquer, transform, and carve a gorge.

THE NECESSITY TO TRANSFORM

In mid summer while resting at the property pond, I observed a caterpillar venture onto a stick that was partially attached to the land, but mostly floating in the water. As the woolly critter inched onto this stick its body weight caused the stick to float away barely off the bank. The caterpillar stopped, it was marooned. In an attempt to escape it moved to the end of the stick, and the stick began to tip into the water, so the caterpillar retreated to the center of the stick. It then moved to the opposite end of the stick, and the tipping repeated. For the second time it retreated to the center of the stick, remaining there, finding balance but not solution. Soon a slight breeze moved the stick back to the bank allowing the caterpillar to reconnect to its comfort zone on land. I thought as I observed the event, this caterpillar will metamorphose into a winged critter offering no challenge to solve its enigma. The caterpillar's transformation is one of the most impressive in nature.

As we transit sticks of life we emulate the caterpillar and its insouciant adventure with the floating stick as we befall displeasure and crisis. We move one direction and things become precarious; we move another direction and the dilemma repeats, discovering balance in the middle. From this point of balance solutions often appear. Sages and spiritual teachers speak of the middle and its importance. Life is a series of adjustments, as we shrug off our past, marching in cadence with the present in a concert of preparation for our impending destiny. From birth to death we are transforming, milestones appear, each a new adventure and also a preparation for events yet to come. Birth, infancy, childhood, puberty, adulthood, aging, and death, reveal transformations. Each chapter offers a unique character, an anthology of experiences, evolving in separate spans of time and space, succumbing to the forces of providence. I am in the aging phase now, and I have observed that during previous phases the pendulum swung with relative uniformity, creating a challenge to construe boundaries from one stage to the next. At this stage of life, the pendulum distinctly slows, clearly defining this transformation period; revealing a culmination of consciousness resulting from life's transit, opening a wellspring of awareness not available when the pendulum was swinging with the vigor of youth.

Observing the world in its present collective state, upheaval and dysfunction are ubiquitous questioning meaningful purpose and direction. Are we an audience in the theatre cheering an empty stage? Is there reason for the chaos? Is it by design or plan? The obscurity of understanding may be an element of transition. We may be in a state of metamorphosis. We may be in the middle of the stick. It is uncertain; however, the necessity to transform is a certainty.

Winter Birds

The insect eaters flee south as harsh winter weather arrives, but certain birds remain, and one must admire these hardy winged folks. The cardinals and blue jays brighten the scene with color, the nuthatch clings to the side of the feeder displaying its agility, there are sparrows, finches, juncos, tufted tit mouse, woodpeckers but my favorite are the chickadees. These tiny birds are astonishing, it can be snowing and blowing and they always make their way to the feeder, often the only species to show up in the severest weather. Austerity is solidly in place this time of year, and to watch the activity surrounding my feeders each day is pure delight.

I have three feeders on the property; two near the house, hanging from the roof on the equipment shed, and one suspended on a pole in the rear next to my cabin. In winter I go through fifty pounds of sunflower seeds and mixed feed each month. They get water from the heated goat and horse troughs. The three feeders are like Grand Central Station, and always a sizable group of juncos hopping around on the ground under the feeders. When the wind blows hard the birds find areas to shelter themselves, under building eves, in thick low lying brushy areas or under the wood pile. They know exactly where to go, true survivors.

Urban dwellers can enjoy the winter birds also, a small feeder in a window can provide a connection with these wonder creatures, but here in this rural zone they are in huge numbers. All of my neighbors are bird feeding enthusiasts, and I noticed at Rural King the amount of bird seed bags are equal in number to the many varieties of livestock feed bags. It truly is one of the great winter pleasures.

The resident flock of crows is a story of their own; they represent the kingpin of the winter birds, on the move from place to place, always in voice and in groups. They glean the corn fields for bits of corn missed by the combine, peck around on the ground near the horses feeding station for spilled grain, check the duck's feeder box to clean up what's left over, and always check the spot where I put broken bread pieces. I buy the low end bread at Wal Mart for .78 cents a loaf, I can't imagine eating this stuff myself but my loquacious, corvid friends think of this bread as a gourmet meal. I do see them on the ground around the feeders, on occasion, picking through the hulls for seeds the feeder bird's drop.

The hunters remain also, I often see the owl or red tailed hawk, and they keep the scale balanced. A small flock of wild turkey wander onto the property and I do wonder exactly what they eat, but imagine the cornfields serve them as they do the crows.

Nature functions with a precision, a repetitive process, adjusting to seasons and weather, a pattern allowing continuation, securing and recognizing the purity, purpose and importance of life. When the spring birds return the mix is greater, and adds to the joys of bird watching. Robins, bluebirds, and barn swallows are among my favorite, but I enjoy them all. There are many fascinating critters to observe in nature, but birds are certainly the most visible, allowing us a connection to them, a relationship that adds a higher dimension to our lives.

An Echo From The Stars

Preparing for winter. It is mid-October and the trees are spectacular. I anticipated autumn to be less colorful. We had such a dry summer; driest of the ten summers I have lived at this place. The pond is very low; we desperately need rain. Early summer rains yielded this radiant scene.

The sun sets earlier now. As the sun lowers it is blocked by trees just west as crimson light filters through open spaces highlighting the eastern side of the property displaying vivid colors of maple, oak and hickory leaves, a dazzling show.

Daily we are inundated with news disclosing a range of events. Politicians posture fabricating exaggerated promises and agendas seeking election with incidents of heroism, medical breakthroughs and social disarray in a profusion of human activity. I often contemplate this unfolding, questioning humankind's presence, purpose and attachment to universal alignment. Global cultural division is widespread although, specific functions are uniform and inspiring, strengthening collective progression toward cohesiveness. Love of family, bonding with nature, embracing spiritual faiths and reproducing displaying idealistic endeavors encouraging meaningful direction. The dark side of humanity is more difficult to understand and assess reason. The horrific evils haunting our species are of no value toward gaining peaceful coexistence and enlightenment. These atrocities are illogical yet continue and often dominate.

The Universe is a mysterious mass; greater understanding emerges as the force of time marches in cadence with cosmic rhythms. The most significant reality is we would not exist without pulsating universal expansion. The Earth is four and a half billion years old, but until the Sun increased in size enabling life to form Earth was barren. One billion years ago early life forms appeared. As I view the magnificence of autumn I think of this. All life on Earth is the result of the Sun's evolution. We are absolutely connected to the Sun, the Universe.

It challenges the mind to comprehend the vastness of the Universe causing tendency to place it secondary. However, combining knowledge and imagination broadens cognition.

Stars have captivated humankind since ancient times. In this modern era many react to star presence in a mundane manner, disregarding significance, casting off universal immensity choosing an approach: "Why bother with something that weaves its fabric with threads in billions when the human tapestry is so small by comparison?" The argument is that small by comparison does not cancel importance. We are important, as important as any particle of matter within universal entirety; thus, should react from this scope of recognition. Universal consciousness adds dimension to the human experience.

Mysterious events have occurred throughout Earth's history. Many such events remain locked in time, undocumented. As we discover physical evidence of these mysteries we fail to comprehend precise understanding of what these revelations represent, infusing modern propensity requiring tangibility. It may be ancient cultures were less distracted, as spiritual bonding with Earth occupied prominence within day-to-day

AN ECHO FROM THE STARS

living designs. The ancients were astute in recognizing the importance of natural functions, they were in awe, attaching to Earth's ebb and flow, dancing with all life, learning to blend and thrive in a world structured with natural blessings, simplistic, earth-born elements, opening opportunity to recognize universal worth.

I was fortunate to attend a series of lectures by futurist Barbara Marx Hubbard in Sarasota, Florida in the mid nineties. Her lectures highlighted humankind's relationship to the Universe. Barbara's theory is present day humanity is in extreme infancy, extrapolating the time span of human existence to the age of the Universe, and the Earth. Science teaches the Universe is in excess of fourteen billion years old, and its ability to expand is likely infinite. Science also reveals humans, similar in stature to humans today have been walking the planet for only 200,000 years. Barbara believes humankind will experience massive changes, suffer horrific events, but ultimately will advance transcending these reversals, continuing to develop as a species, attaining a zenith at a much higher position than present day. If we have developed to this point in 200,000 years, imagine what we will become in a billion years. As we know, change jumps to the quantum. This is the crux of Barbara's message, as we gain closer time relationship to the Universe we will grow more intensely connected to its overall force and purpose. In her view, we are primitive, compared to subsequent evolutionary transformations. The ubiquity of hate, wars and inequality will dissipate, gaining ability to transcend higher within ourselves, extending compassion, embracing complexities with greater knowledge resulting in more profound togetherness and significance.

There is also evidence of star connections on Earth in physical form, and as difficult as this is to grasp it is also difficult to ignore. Located in South America are long road-like lines, displaying symbolic images and designs only recognizable from high altitudes. There is a lake, named in ancient times "Rabbit Lake", displaying a rabbit's image, only detectable at 3000 feet in altitude.

The Pyramids were largely ignored for over 3000 years, until the Greeks took interest in them. Modern archeologists have been astounded by certain findings relating to the Pyramids. These are very large structures, and measurements from corner to corner are within six-inch tolerances. Large, modern buildings, not nearly the sizes of the Pyramids, are unable to attain this architectural tolerance ability. The Egyptians, during the pyramid construction era, had no pulley or wheel systems available to maneuver such large blocks of stone, which were quarried across the Nile, then moved to the construction site and the Pyramid's internal main shafts align perfectly with the star Sirius, causing wonder. Some historians theorize that the Pyramids were not originally constructed as tombs, but ultimately used as tombs. The irony is from the time beyond the Pyramid construction era tombs were constructed in a more conventional manner in the Valley of the Kings.

When the Pyramids were new they were finished smooth, shined in sunlight, and had capstones. Modern science is unable to explain the complete history or purpose of the Pyramids.

One compelling detail has emerged. An ancient tribe of people, the Dogon, migrated to West Africa from Egypt. Their origin is from the vicinity of the Pyramids during the Pyramid construction period. According to Dogon tradition, the star

AN ECHO FROM THE STARS

Sirius has a companion star, which is also depicted in ancient Dogon cave drawings. This star is invisible to the naked eye, but the Dogon had knowledge of this star and also knew it orbits Sirius every 50 years. Two French anthropologists _ Marcel Grianule and Germain Dieterlen _ recorded this from a Dogon priest in 1930. How could an ancient tribe lacking astronomical devices have knowledge of an invisible star? They also knew Jupiter had four major moons and Sirius's small companion star was extremely dense, as science would later discover. One teaspoon of matter from this tiny star would weigh 5 tons on Earth. The star, which scientists eventually named Sirius B, was not officially seen or recorded until the late nineteenth century when telescopes were developed enough allowing visual identification. It was not photographed until 1970.

According to Dogon ancient oral history a race of people from the Sirius system called Nommas visited the Earth. They also appear in Babylonian, Acadian, and Sumerian myths. According to Dogon legend the Nommas lived on a planet that orbits another star in the Sirius system. They landed on the Earth in an ark that made a spinning decent to the ground with great noise and wind. It was the Nommas who gave the Dogon knowledge of Sirius B, and may have been responsible for Pyramid construction. The Sirius system is close in proximity to Earth, eight light years, and in comparison to the depth of the Universe a 20-minute commute. The furthest known distance in our Universe is thirteen billion light years, a fascinating comparison.

What can these revelations possibly mean, and how can - or does - it affect people of modern times? Much can be hypothesized compounding into various assessments. The ancients serve as our guides; we are their reflection, as we may be to those who replace us in 100,000 years. Looking at the ancients more closely, the Neanderthals represent an interesting beginning. Anthropologists tell us beings much like ourselves were first known of 200,000 years ago and called MHS (modern human species). Yet, earlier species appeared before MHS and among the earliest were the Neanderthal: their history goes back 500,000 years. They were a bit different, smaller, stoutly built, had short life spans, around thirty years; yet, they represent much more. Modern times characterize Neanderthals as dull-witted, slow thinking, lacking creativeness, with low-level mental processing ability. Nothing could be further from the truth. The Neanderthal depicted the essence of the human spirit exhibiting extraordinary ability to rise to challenge and adversity. The Neanderthal's brain was larger than modern humans, but science tells us their brains functioned differently, enhancing capacity to calculate basic survival rudiments, manufacture tools directly from the Earth, learning to hunt, gather food, fabricate clothing from animal skins, assimilating with Earth more profoundly than any form of human beyond their time. They migrated from Africa to what is now Europe, and went as far north to what is now Russia. They adjusted to various conditions, enduring extreme cold thriving in high, harsh latitudes, an amazing feat. I have spent blocks of time in wilderness areas using modern, high-tech equipment and the conditions are often challenging. To imagine starting from nothing, it is astonishing to think how they were able to endure extreme climatic conditions. Yet they did, exemplifying how diverse and adaptable humans can be. Neanderthals disappeared 40,000 years ago, and anthropologists surmise the MHS eventually moved into the regions occupied by Neanderthal, and a form of bonding or destruction occurred resulting in their demise. This is theory specifics remain a mystery.

Envisioning the immensity of the Universe, comparing it to our individual lives, we seem miniscule. However, as our lives open to higher dimensions of consciousness we become flecks of gold in the prospector's pan. As we sluice gravel from the creek we are given, representing our time on Earth, the nuggets we find are where we discover love of life and recognition, not only displaying contemporary purpose; we reflect the past and project the future. We are the Neanderthal, we are the modern, new, high-tech species; the gardeners that grow the wheat feeding the next generation, which moves forward replicating life's ever-present energy.

In 1970, I lived at another place, also rural. My neighbor, Mr. Davis, lived across the road. He was in his 80's when I met him. I visited him at his house where he was born and lived with his sister his entire life. He invited me in, proudly showing me a photo album dating to the early years of the twentieth century, showing him during the only time he had not lived in this house, when he was a soldier in WWI. I was so enthralled. We then sat on his porch and had tea, and I mentioned how beautiful the big hardwoods surrounding his house were. These were mature trees. Mr. Davis told me he planted these trees as a boy. I imagined a young boy planting seedlings that were now majestic giants. This experience offered awakening that we can and do leave a mark as we traverse life. He also told me of a tornado in 1910 knocking all the windows out of his house. The property where my house is located was a cabin and it was destroyed. My house was built in 1911 and Mr. Davis, in his youth, watched the carpenters work each day.

 A few of us will make the century mark. Most won't, but it's of less importance how long we live than what we do with time given. It was late evening when I left Mr. Davis's porch, the moon was shining through his big oak tree. As I walked across the field to my house, stars filled the sky and I found Orion. It was a sensuous moment. I then squinted my eyes looking skyward, seeing the stars in a diffused blur, and it seemed I could hear an echo.

Shadows of Time

In the early 60's I lived and worked in Detroit. During this time Detroit was an active, vibrant and thriving metropolis not the hollow place it is today. As I drove to work daily I passed a small deli at 5AM; the light was on, they opened each morning at 6AM. Inside two figures were moving about in preparation for the day's business. I habitually had lunch at this small deli and they served corned beef sandwiches like I had never experienced before or since. Each sandwich was cut to order and served hot on a choice of exquisite breads, baked nightly by a neighboring business, the Carrini family Italian bakery. This was a small place, a counter, with a few stools, tables and chairs, simplistic and immaculately clean and orderly. The proprietors were two elderly folks, man and wife. They emitted brightness with constant smiles and friendly greetings. This kind of place is not commonly found today, it's a different world now, as we approach plastic counters with uniformed employees greeting us like trained seals, programmed, infusing synthetic, corporate sincerity and politeness. This deli couple amazed me; they seemed connected by an invisible filament as they jointly performed daily tasks. The wife was the greeter, waitress and cashier, and the husband was the cook and dishwasher. They both mopped the floor and cleaned the restrooms. They opened each day at 6AM, and closed at 7PM, with an hour's work after closing, 6 days a week. As I conversed with them I noticed each had a tattoo on their forearms, a series of numbers that were beginning to fade with time. Of course there was no need to ask their significance, these were symbolic of a dark time in their lives, as I wondered how they could show such joy in the present.

As we transit the path of life, we each follow a certain light, a beacon, leading us forward to unknown and mysterious places, casting shadows of our past. Our shadows are on shelves in pictures, or in boxes stored in attics and basements, and sometimes we visit, as we drift back and touch these shadows with our minds. Over the many years I have often thought of that Jewish couple, how they embraced their work with such grace. To imagine what horrors their minds held, what their memories must contain, from a time when the world lived in a long dark shadow that seemed perpetual.

There is darkness now, but as I compare present complexities to the time of the deli couple they seem miniscule. Our culture has fallen into a trap of ease and comfort; few today feel the wrath of deep and punishing hardship, as those two beautiful people had known. They were young when they were imprisoned; yet, they rose again and faced the world head on, extracting what they could, always feeling the presence of their shadows as they moved forward to a new light. Can we emulate such grace; discover new meaning and purpose as we transit the labyrinthine of our future? It is our responsibility. It can be done.

The Puzzlement of Ancient Spirituality

Comparing ancient living design to modern society is a study in contrast. Archeological discoveries reveal ancient cultures imposed greater communal value on spirituality. This evidence is compelling and may provide a window of opportunity for contemporary recurrence toward social harmony prevalent during early eras of human development.

Petroglyphs are ancient artistic rock carvings depicting daily life. Stonehenge and the giant Moai of Easter Island are examples of spiritually induced artifacts. Early societies were influenced by virtue of transcendent energy fusing with Earth's natural pulse yielding a sense of connection, worth and belonging. Nature's benevolence remains but less intensely recognized lacking reverence displayed by the ancients. We crowd to view natural wonders, enjoying mountain vistas, highlighting scenic importance but largely absent of spiritual connection.

How exactly were ancient cultures more spiritually absorbed in osmosis with Earth's natural power and magnitude? A thought worthy question.

Populations expanded, shifting values and living order to a new plane. This caused radical change in social goals. The ancients were sparse and widely scattered forming cohesive tribal units. As human presence enlarged it required complex governments, border establishments resulting in possessiveness and restrictive laws blocking intrinsic processes to gain necessities for life. Agriculture converted into a co-operative effort, forming monetary systems to obtain food. Ownership and fiscal value were attached to basic shelter moving beyond sanctuary, becoming exhibitions of wealth and social division. Ancient societies implemented housing uniformly arranged using simplistic designs, placing function above vanity.

Theses changSo, these changes fueled evolution to current social position. This new direction developed into large-scale conflicts and eventual amassing invasive armies driven to gain dominance and control expanding this more complex cultural scheme titling it civilization, distancing from primitive influence and profound spirituality present during earlier historic times.

es prompt the question: "Are we better off?" Some would argue we are, as luxury and comfort combines with materialism reaching far beyond necessity. During winter months when I observe a Rose Breasted Grosbeak perched on my feeder flaunting its intense beauty, magnified by the white snowy background, I feel enlightened connecting with this magnificent being of nature. When cash pops out of the slot at the ATM spiritual thoughts do not appear. Only a piercing message that I now must use my cash to attain brown rice, bottled water and gasoline or I will perish. Logically we are capable of renewing collective spirituality, challenged to navigate distractions absent during ancient times. As members of this new species we may fail to rediscover the symmetrical formation the ancients shared with the Earth; however, asymmetry offers

THE PUZZLEMENT OF ANCIENT SPIRITUALITY

balance also, and often with greater integrity. Individually we can mirror ancient spirituality by stepping around modern social barriers. Introspective vitality remains obtainable, and as we take a day or month we can re-establish cadence with those of long ago, embracing natural beauty, extending its power deep into our hearts and souls.

Spirituality exhibited in early times can serve as our savior. We feel a sense of bonding learning and assimilating ancient ways, evidenced individually and through group efforts during these modern times forming redirection toward natural earthly functions. Newness is emerging. Foods are trending toward less processed choices. Environmental preservation is moving to the forefront finding new direction toward an improved world, solving the puzzle of the ancients, and applying these practices to modern spiritual pursuits opening wider dimensions to our lives.

The voice of destiny sings in various rhythmic tones, often off key and out of tempo, like a catbird singing in a thorn bush. Then the sky opens and darkness become light as clouds of doubt vanish.

Nature Speaking

The dew glistens when the sun strikes the pasture adding sparkle to the sunrise causing a visual tweak to this new day. My attendance gives in to the language of such a morning. This early voice of nature harmonizes with contrasting tones of green grass and blue sky as the silence speaks in softness. In the shaded woods the May apple spreads its fan of leaves low, in clusters of spring delight seeding quickly to be gone by summer. They are the essence of this season an ephemeral, sacred plant. Seeing such beauty each day mirrors nature's splendor gazing back in a guiding light from worldly chaos. The puissance of nature is ever-present releasing power through its array of organisms, forgiving and unforgiving; yet, balanced in perfect cadence with Earth's rhythms and cycles.

The morning silence is cracked by a flock of boisterous crows transiting the pasture's sky in silhouetted motion with destination only known to them. Scattered white clouds mix with the deep blue sky, a backdrop for the crow's stage at this early hour.

With all its power nature is also delicate, ravaged, exemplified by humankind's drive to install the crisp hum of a new power line, or a road to accommodate commuters. Soon thereafter comes the horrid clatter of bulldozers followed by concrete trucks as human expansion overpowers nature's benevolence. Preservation is quelled by pursuit of convenience

NATURE SPEAKING

and comfort; it's a disheartening reality of our times. The social distancing from the lessons and beauty of nature has proven to be a place of confusion and despair, communally gearing downward, plagued by the clutter of gadgets. Squalor and wealth form boundaries of separation creating class distinction, a structure without structure. There is subtraction here, a loss of individuality, as the social order grows toward automated reliance, a noisy place, confining, as the cage of urbanization closes its door. A cell is formed dictated by economic and material forces, inundating, blocking introspection, as the pulse of consumption grows ever louder squelching the quiet charity of simplicity.

Yesterday at the pond I observed the first years sighting of the water snake. I didn't see it last year, was worried it had perished. However, they are difficult to see in an idle state and I likely overlooked its presence. It gracefully moved across the pond's surface, allowing me the pleasure of this sighting. Many are horrified of snakes, and I do wonder why this is. These are creatures of the Earth, they are important to the ecosystem, quite amazing life forms, move with stealth and elegance, using natural gifts to thrive among the challenges nature offers. I also saw a big snapper on land, my guess its a female laying her eggs. You seldom see these turtles their lives are aquatic, but early summer brings them to the land to lay their eggs. If one takes time to observe nature's functions an attachment is formed, an understanding. A love bond grows. It's an element that is not available to those trapped in the stench of cities as noise and polluted air cloaks enchantment of wild places.

Humankind's future is in question. Improvements from earlier times reveal signs of hope. We don't slaughter wild animals into extinction as we once did. Human slavery and child labor are gone and gender bias has dissipated. The largest challenge looming is our sheer numbers, and the ongoing provocations leading to war. Our species must comply and adjust in a higher fashion to Earth's tempo, moving toward nature as opposed to away from it. It does seem possible; however, also worrisome pondering the consequences if we cannot.

          Hinterland

Remembering Uncle J.P.

(Autobiographical essay)

I lived in Vienna, West Virginia until age eleven, we then moved to Marion, Ohio where I entered sixth grade in 1951. Formative years unveil perpetual newness.

Industrial states felt economic surge in the early forties created from war demands while West Virginia remained stalled; although, industrialized states struggled during The Great Depression era whereas West Virginia remained as it had always been. The thirties were more of a speed bump than a crisis since the state historically functioned on a fiscal precipice. However, my parents and grandparents were above the poverty line.

I attended Vienna School grades one through five, built in the nineteenth century with oiled wood floors, suspended globe lamps, wooden desks with inkwells and lift tops to store books, also paddles hanging next to blackboards. We didn't change rooms, one teacher taught all subjects, but did changed rooms twice a week for music and on Fridays when our principal Mr. Huffman showed a movie in the largest classroom. We crowded in, some standing, to watch a 16mm, black-and-white film. I remember two, Destination Moon and One Million BC. I distinctly remember One Million BC as I was overcome with fear watching cave men fight dinosaurs, later learning dinosaurs were extinct millions of years before humans appeared. Teachers were the most memorable, all women, very strict and although paddles were seldom used they played a symbolic role as reminders disruption would not be tolerated. It was an interesting time to experience youth. Difficult to imagine such conditions today as parents closely monitor teacher activity. Stern discipline has been removed from schools. Contemporary educational systems mail parents neatly typed and carefully composed correspondence detailing disruptive behavior and a meeting is scheduled to politely discuss incidents of disruption. At Vienna School in the forties teachers clarified issues on site, quickly and effectively.

My grandparents on my mother's side, the Slater's, lived in Parkersburg, six miles from Vienna and we visited frequently. My grandfather Slater was retired; during working years he sold cemetery lots. The Slater's were vagabonds of sorts, they owned a small orange grove in California in the early twentieth century and I remember old photographs of this farm. Grandfather Slater had taken a job in San Francisco traveling from Georgia. His wife Minnie arrived a year later by train with three children. They were married in Claxton, Georgia in 1902. Grandfather Slater lived in San Francisco during the earthquake and fire destroying the city in 1906, before Minnie arrived. He was a handsome man, performed skits in vaudeville shows and had a variety of jobs, somehow ending up with the orange grove. I am without knowledge regarding reasons for moving to Parkersburg, WV, but my mother went to Parkersburg High School graduating in 1930. I remember seeing a photograph taken in California

REMEMBERING UNCLE J.P.

showing three children with my grandparents. One was my Aunt Sadie and one, Clara, who died during childhood, and also pictured was a small, wide-eyed boy standing tall, and this was my uncle J.P., born in 1903. My mother Helen was born in 1911 and was not in this photo. I also had an Aunt Janet, born a year before my mother; Aunt Janet was the academic of the family, graduating from Parkersburg High School in 1929 as class salutatorian. My Uncle Bill was the youngest, unsure of his birth year, it must have been around 1920 since he had graduated from high school prior to being drafted into the army in 1941. Uncle Bill was the most charismatic member of the family, very good looking and gregarious, everyone was drawn to him, he possessed all the natural gifts. He was comfortable in social settings, became a hero in Italy during combat with the Germans and awarded the Bronze Star for bravery enhancing his charisma. Everyone loved uncle Bill.

Uncle J. P. (James Paxton, Jr.), everyone called him J.P., was too old to be drafted and suffered from a mild learning disability, not classified as retarded but a slow learner and was removed from school after the fifth grade. No special education classes in those days. Uncle J.P. was bullied and shunned socially at school, likely contributing to poor academic performance. The Uncle J.P. I knew was anything but a slow learner, he was smart, read the newspaper front to back each day, and knew more than most realized.

Uncle J.P. lived at home with my grandparents, Jim and Minnie. Uncle Bill and Uncle J.P. displayed vividly contrasting personalities. In the course of daily life my grandfather habitually imposed verbal humiliation directed at uncle J.P., hurtful snipes exaggerating minor issues. When Uncle Bill visited he contributed to this activity. Even at my young age this made me uncomfortable and I knew it was wrong. I came to love Uncle J.P., so much; he paid more attention to me than other adults in the family, often reading me newspaper articles. Uncle J.P. was also a master gardener; he knew everything one could possibly know about gardening. His garden was large, centering his life. He sold sweet corn, tomatoes and strawberries. People came from great distances to buy his produce. His garden was organic and perfect. He marinated tobacco in water then put this mixture in a garden sprayer using it as a pesticide. I was impressed at the neatness of his rows; always weed free as he worked tirelessly with his hoe in the sun wearing a straw hat. To escape verbal abuse uncle J.P. stayed to himself leading a solitary life. He told me he saved one hundred dollars, which I thought was a huge amount of money. Parkersburg High School was nearby, and Uncle J.P. volunteered to chalk the yard lines on the field for home football games. He did this for years, and coaches and players came to know and love him. They treated him better than anyone; he so enjoyed this job, representing his only social connection allowing a sense of worth and importance. They gave him a permanent pass, but he always returned home and listened to the games on the radio.

 The torment from family members damaged Uncle J.P., but he concealed his feelings. Uncle J.P. smoked all day and Grandfather Slater and Uncle Bill were also heavy drinkers, fueling their abuse toward Uncle J.P. Uncle J.P. never used alcohol, had very little money, and would hand roll cigarettes on a small hand crank machine. His thumb and forefinger on his right hand were yellow with stain from smoking cigarettes. The family was not totally dysfunctional, they shared meals, and there were times of harmonious interaction, but love was shallow and much of the food was from the garden and never a word of praise directed at Uncle J.P. for his effort.

When I was around ten I remember Uncle J.P. holding his hand over his heart complaining of pain. He was told that it was indigestion. Later, I remember my mother getting a phone call, and she began to cry. We were living in Ohio then, and drove directly to Parkersburg to my grandparent's house. Uncle J.P. had shot himself in the head with my grandfather's revolver. He was not dead, but mortally wounded and at the hospital. I had never felt such emotional pain, it hit me so hard, it seemed I would surely die. They brought Uncle J.P. home and rented a hospital bed, he was in a coma and his head was badly swollen, he died three days later. Uncle Bill, my grandfather and grandmother were overcome with grief manifested from guilt. From the time they brought Uncle J.P. home from the hospital Uncle Bill remained at his bedside, would not leave, eat or sleep, staring at Uncle J.P. the entire time until his death. This incident caused family breakdown, complete devastation, and everyone wept uncontrollably displaying suffering I was unfamiliar with at my early age.

This was a harsh lesson in life. These experiences caused me to open an extra portion of my heart to those I observe who are shunned or emotionally damaged from the treatment of others. Uncle J.P. was a magnificent person, he was kind to everyone, never complained, ever, and loved plants and nature in all its forms. Few people ever attain the level of connection to the Earth Uncle J.P. achieved. I did not recognize this until adulthood, but the pain I felt at the funeral home, observing my grandparents and Uncle Bill overcome with intense grief has never left my memory. They were broken. It was 1953; Uncle J.P. was fifty years old.

All of those of that generation of my family are gone now. Uncle Bill died of a heart attack at age fifty-six, associated with alcoholism and heavy tobacco use. Observing him throughout his later years he seemed empty. He wrote me letters while I was in the USMC. Often these letters reflected his youth and I remember him telling me how he and Uncle J.P. played together as kids. They loved baseball but no baseball diamonds were near and they began playing stickball on a vacant lot using a broomstick and a rubber ball. After a time, the rubber ball split down the middle, leaving two halves, and since they could not afford another ball they began playing with one half. They soon discovered it was more fun than when the ball was whole, jumping around when pitched, doing crazy things when hit, eventually giving the game a name calling it "half-rubber". Kids would gather for a game of "half-rubber". Uncle Bill thought this might be a marketable game, but never ventured beyond a thought. It was sad to read uncle Bill's letters describing his memories of Uncle J.P. One would think with Uncle Bill's broad experiences, war heroism, and life's interactions brought forth from social gifts, those experiences would remain prominent in his memory. His memory of playing stickball with his older brother found its way to the forefront. Often, simplistic, less grand events flash forward with clarity as aging descends.

Families' falling down frequently occurs, spiraling into darkness. Recollecting my uncle and grandfather intimidating

REMEMBERING UNCLE J.P.

Uncle J. P., my thoughts are: "What if Uncle J.P. tried to retaliate, resist and fight back?" He couldn't, he did not possess an anger-based, confrontational demeanor, he also had no place to go being poorly educated and not easily accepted socially. His only job skill was gardening. Uncle J.P. was in a cage of despair, and my uncle and grandfather were poking sticks at him. Viewing this through the eyes of a child is indelible; I thought Uncle J.P. was a glorious, compassionate person, never critical toward others.

I recently returned to Parkersburg for a visit. Slater's house was demolished and the large lot where Uncle J.P created his beautiful garden was weed infested with abandoned cars occupying this space. The picture in my mind reminisced a gentle man hoeing weeds on a hot summer day. Time gauges life, stirring emotions ranging from joy to sadness. Memories cling like shadows.

I am seventy-three now and feel blessed to remain. Awareness that the average US male life expectancy is seventy-three weighs on my mind, but also adds dimension seizing reverence each day unfolds. I live with my two dogs Orion and Venus in a small cabin, five hundred feet from the lightly traveled road, on fourteen rural acres of pasture, pond and woods, an introspective place. This is where I will likely remain the duration of my life.

There is freshness on this cool, late February morning and high in the sky is a flock of the sand-hill cranes trumpeting in their flight north signaling the cusp of spring. Nature displays balanced perfection. Humankind is plagued with misdirection, struggling within itself, drifting in continual disharmony. It is a hope that as a species we will evolve to more congruity.

HINTERLAND JOURNAL

The voice of destiny sings in various rhythmic tones, often off key and out of tempo, like a catbird singing in a thorn bush. Then the sky opens and darkness becomes light as clouds of doubt vanish. On this special pre-spring day I am remembering Uncle J.P.

Techno Logic

I recently received an e-mail message with an attached photo exhibiting a group of soldiers proudly surrounding a newly developed "bunker busting" bomb. The text of the message explained this was no ordinary bomb, constructed using state of the art technology; capable of destroying the most heavily fortified military bunkers. Praising this weapon reflects historical propensity for fusing technological resources with tools of war.

As modern technology assumes social prominence questions arise. Young people obsessed with incessant cell phone chatting and entranced by fantasy imagery depicting violent video games. Computer hackers use technology as a theft device. Privacy invasion and child exploitation are ubiquitous and expanding. These practices form social contractions. So, the finger of accountability is pointed at technology as the monster, which is an unjust accusation. Technology has self-replicated since inception. The monster is, and always has been, humanity itself. Thievery, privacy invasion and child exploitation existed long before computer development. However, modern technology intensifies method, range and ability. Communally we are challenged to orient technology on a more beneficial course.

Imagining discovery of fire, revealing power beyond any previously known. It is plausible tribal members pointed at fire and spoke of its danger and potential for devastation, how it would destroy and consume them. The ancients discovered they could warm their bodies and cook food by controlling fire. Applications of fire revealed ability to enhance or destroy life. Technologically induced power historically kindles apprehension and fear often wending toward war applications. War is humankind's most profound nemesis. Futurists predict over great spans of time war will become extinct. Presently war remains steadfast and eminent.

In a recent issue of Orion Magazine appeared a thought-provoking essay titled Dark Ecology written by Paul Kingsnorth. This essay addressed convolution within environmental movements softening to destructive impact on ecosystems. These observations are valid and worrisome; however, influential goals remain achievable, capable of altering negative intrusion. Government interventions are plagued with missteps and fiscal bumbling providing minimal change. Corruptive forces frequently infiltrate and victimize organizations fueled by subversive power of money. If we seek solutions only via political means perplexity will prevail continuing to produce fragmented results. Technical applications can serve as pathfinders discovering methods of environmental healing and preservation. Combining knowledge with communication divulges power for change and no time in history have these two entities been so readily at hand. Knowledge and communication share a road with creativity. This cogent trio can enliven workable solutions beyond legislative efforts. Change can also manifest naturally through habitual, selective individual choices through local cooperatives, transcending the awkwardness of organizational efforts.

TECHNO LOGIC

Paul Kingsnorth's fine essay defines the ancient scythe as a superior tool to the motorized brush cutter. I also use a scythe on my property for cutting weeds and agree with Paul it is a superior tool to the motorized cutter and more soulful to use. Ecological management and nature's preservation benefits from hands on efforts in unison with technology. As efficient as my scythe is, it cannot cut close to buildings, trees and fence posts as the motorized unit can with ease. It's a splendid example of blending old technology with new.

Technology's bright side is inspiring and gratifying. My home is in an isolated, rural location and the nearby hamlet is a microcosmic habitat. One resident is a paraplegic man who travels about mobilized using his highly technical motorized wheelchair. He visits the post office each morning, waves at passers bys, stops at the store and spends time at the small park. He enjoys discussing his wheelchair, explaining how it has opened his life to a broader dimension. When I contemplate this young man's life without his wheelchair I envision an empty space, a small room with minimal human interaction. His life is expanded and fulfilled because of a technological device. Medical technology has enhanced lives in a myriad of ways, playing important roles improving daily functions for those with disabilities.

A respected scholar, author and environmentalist wrote an essay on why he does not own a computer. This essay made little sense to me. From my view it would be like an ancient Persian gardener writing an essay explaining why he does not own a hoe. Modern day attachment to technology reveals a garden of change, imposing intricacies plagued with weeds and vermin. Cyber thieves and child exploiters can only be eradicated using capable and equal methods. The computer is our hoe.

Government agencies and large-scale environmental movements have made some significant contributions. When I was growing up in the forties and early fifties I lived in a small town near the Ohio River. During this time the Ohio River was heavily polluted from dumping industrial waste directly into the river. Today the Ohio River is a much cleaner body of water because of government intervention and enforcement. The downside to government agencies is that change is slow and difficult, hindered by political posturing, influential lobby groups and dissention within leadership ranks. Individually it is difficult to implement sweeping changes upon industrial activity, which is considered a social necessity. However, personal choices can influence positive change toward overall betterment. The power of the people remains a force beyond what is typically perceived.

During the nineteenth and early twentieth centuries vast exploitation of natural resources transpired. Widespread environmental devastation was an accepted standard. Train passengers traveling west were entertained by shooting buffalo from the train's windows, leaving thousands of carcasses to rot in the sun. Millions of passenger pigeons were slaughtered using nets and mass shootings, causing eventual extinction of this magnificent bird that once numbered in excess of three billion. Redwood forests were clear-cut by lumber barons. Hydraulic gold mining desecrated landscapes driven by a quest for wealth. These horrid displays of destructive behavior demonstrated an absence of compassion, void of perseveration's importance. We have advanced from such behavior; we

TECHNO LOGIC

don't senselessly slaughter wild animals into extinction now or clear-cut redwood trees, and these positive changes are a result of social refinements. In these modern times the most vexing problem is our sheer numbers, a glaring issue.

Fossil fuel is globally ingrained creating a source for atmospheric pollution. As population and consumption increases need for fossil fuel also increases, forming a conundrum. Social design places economics at the forefront. Political candidates will not acquire votes discussing pollutants or energy alternatives. This taints the notion that government agencies offer solutions. What we do have is advancement of technological enterprise seeking and finding alternative energy sources displaying genuine and practical applications, with some presently in place. Technology bonding with creative enterprise may be our best approach. Technology eventually will prove significance to the "Holy Grail" of fiscal leverage awakening voters to the worth of environmentally friendly alternatives. Nothing is more important than a healthy environment. Earth, and its inhabitants form a singular organism with health standing alone as a priority. Life and a continuation of life is the natural process carrying us to the present. Technology may help discover solutions insuring perpetuity of life on planet Earth. It is techno-logical.

CPSIA information can be obtained at www.ICGtesting.com
Printed in the USA
LVOW06s0119031214

416537LV00001B/38/P

9 781478 742951